THE WALKING DOCTOR

By Lucienne LeBeau

This book is a work of fiction. Names, characters, places, and incidents either are products of the author's imagination or used fictitiously. Any resemblance to actual events or locales and persons, living or dead, is entirely coincidental.

The author is now fairly sure locales can be dead if they're ghost towns.

2nd Edition © 2024 by Silver Hollow Stories, LLC. Printed by Ascendant Publishing with permission grom the author.

Edited by Michael Strong

Cover Art by Michael Strong

Special thanks to Yuri_B and Pixabay.com

For more information and to purchase Lucienne's other works, visit silverhollowstories.com or ascendantpublishing.com.

Thanks to Michael as always. This book is dedicated to my father and his love of westerns and horror.

FOREWORD

This is a Weird West tale that takes place in the Silver Hollow Universe. It's not necessary to have read the Silver Hollow trilogy, but it does feature a certain character those readers might find familiar. While she is not exactly the same person, she is a possibility. If you've read my other work, then you know I love to explore possibilities. In the four years since I wrote this, I think you'll find what I wrote about it four years ago to be important for what we've faced this year, and what we face during any kind of epidemic or pandemic.

Bear in mind that this work of mine is 100% a work of fiction. Virology and immunology are incredible sciences, and though I did do quite a bit of literature review, I just couldn't fit our world's reality into my world's fantasy. But in this case, science is a necessary foundation to the story, but it is secondary.

Real science—the kind of work that has nearly eradicated polio, destroyed smallpox, and given us beautiful ways to cope with the human condition—takes decades of hard work and entire teams of people. The beauty of science is not in a single genius virologist or someone working in isolation to discover a cure for a disease—the beauty is in the teamwork and the discoveries made through the scientific process.

I take enormous liberties with diseases and viruses, and if you're any kind of expert, you'll see things that might make you pause and question, but remember that here, things are vastly different than in the real world. Terra and Earth seem a lot alike, but there are keen differences that make it fun. I hope.

I'd like to thank my friend Jay Willison for his help teaching me about firearms (all mistakes and liberties are mine and mine alone), and to Michael Strong, for all the support and saving this manuscript from being eaten by the cloud.

And in this 2nd Edition hardcover, I would like to thank my friend and brother from another mother, Wally Quigley, my mad scientist buddy.

So welcome again to my world, dear reader. Please take my hand and don't let go, because I know the way out.

Lucienne LeBeau

June 30, 2024

Atlanta, Georgia, USA

THE WALKING DOCTOR

Hardpan beneath once-black boots covered in a layer of dust. Spurs jingled with every step. The doctor's feet sent daggers of pain through long legs and up the spine. A plea to stop, a plea to rest.

This doctor kept walking, pushing through each burning toe, each blistering heel, soles aflame. A gun on the hip, a satchel on the back, a locket and vial around the neck, near the heart.

The heels of the boots on the hardpan echoed with dull clacks. Ahead, on the horizon, a network of foothills scraped at the enormous blue sky.

A hot wind picked up and the walking doctor pulled a bandana over nose and mouth, pushing a pair of shade-spectacles up the bridge of the nose.

Kathryn Judge cocked her head and stopped walking. It looked like she was trying to figure out a puzzle, but she was listening.

Help us, oh please won't someone help us—

I can't stand to see him suffer like this—

We need a doctor; time is running out—

The physician sighed and ran a hand over her forehead. Listening brought nosebleeds. Nosebleeds brought questions.

"Questions I can't answer," she said to the town on the horizon. It was nestled against the foothills, near water. Kathryn closed her mouth and walked again.

You're a stubborn girl, and you'll be a tenacious woman, her mother's voice said in her mind. With every step, her mind gave way to her past. She could still picture the pineapple sitting in the center of the table as she stood with her arms folded, glaring at her mother. The anger she felt that day was now long gone, but she remembered how the older woman took it: with grace. That's a good trait to have, Kit, and it'll come in handy when you're facing the razor. Now go upstairs and get dressed and we'll discuss it after the party. I promise.

She smiled. Her mother had kept true to her word. Once the pineapple was taken off the table and the guests made their leave, her mother talked to her long and hard about boarding school in Albion.

The tenacity never faded, and that's how she kept putting one foot in front of the other, even through aching heels and burning toes. Mile after mile of walking made her boots too tight. Five pounds of sausage in a three-pound casing.

This journey might be worth it, it might not. Kathryn kept looking ahead, and then in front of her. On the lookout for snakes, for scorpions. None of them were stupid enough to be out in such heat. Only humans were willing to be that (tenacious) unwise.

Perhaps this was an ill-advised journey, but she kept walking. There was no point in turning back now.

As she moved, the locket made a light clack against the vial, and Kathryn frowned under her bandana. One hand moved over it to separate them, to lay them better over her heart.

Once the wind settled, the doctor pulled down the cloth back around her neck and took a deep breath. The air carried a scent that tugged on her memories—days of dry summers during the Charles Town drought of 1876, when Papa said they'd make the best of the day. The scent of a barbecue, and roasted corn. Crackles of pig fat and fluffy clouds overhead, promising a rain that wouldn't come for a fortnight.

Dry, rough lips, cracked from the sun, opened as if they could take a taste of the air, then closed again. Running low on water, Kathryn looked ahead, then checked her bearings. By her map and compass, the Twist River was just ahead to the northwest, about half a day of walking if she kept her current pace.

A cart with an awning, converted from a covered wagon, grew bigger as the doctor kept walking. The scents of summer strengthened as she drew near. The lure of food and drink for a hungry traveler was more than Kathryn could bear, and her feet carried her towards the wagon-cart.

"You hungry, tall stranger?" The woman asked. She was a smaller woman than Kathryn—came up to the physician's chest, and her long, weathered face had lines around the eyes that told the doc the smile she was wearing was almost permanent.

Kathryn managed a small smile and nodded. "Hungry, thirsty."

"We got whiskey, got buffalo, and corn. You got barter?" The woman threw her chin towards Kathryn's satchel.

The doctor nodded. "Got beads, got gold, got paper money. How much for a plate and a glass?"

"Paper money? Thought you sounded like you were from Away." The older woman chuckled. "One half-dollar and I'll let you have two plates and five glasses."

Kathryn reached into her satchel and took a quick glance around at the area. No one but her and the older lady. She pulled out a dollar and handed it over. "You got water?"

"Fresh from the Twist. I'll let you fill your canteen—the dollar's more than enough." The woman with the silver-stranded braids turned to the side to show Kathryn the iron cauldron, presumably filled with water. "First, you come sit and eat. Where's your horse?"

Kathryn shook her head. "I don't ride."

"Don't know how?"

"Don't deserve a horse." Kit squinted behind her shade-spectacles and though the older woman couldn't see her eyes, she dropped the subject. It was in her tone.

"You got a name?"

"Doesn't everyone?"

At this, the older woman laughed. "I suppose they do eventually. My name's Yaja." She put her hand over her heart and bowed her head forward so Kathryn could see the red-brown scalp at her perfect hair part.

"Kathryn Judge. You can call me Kit." Kathryn returned the gesture, with one hand over her heart, fingers brushing over the lump the locket and vial made under her yellowing shirt.

"Well, Kit, it's a long way from back East. Sit. Eat. Rest."

Yaja fixed Kit a plate of buffalo brisket, corn, beans, and tack bread. She gestured with the plate in one hand and a tall glass of whiskey in the other. "Have a seat at that barrel. Eat up."

Kathryn thanked her and sat in a chair at the edge of an upturned spool used for laying cable. A long awning over the chair and makeshift table provided some much-needed shade. The woman named Yaja was close by, standing at the grill under the side awning. The scents of sweet and savory tinged the air, and with a rumbling stomach, she tucked in and let the corn on the cob pop into her mouth as though she hadn't eaten in days. Maybe she hadn't. There were times the days ran all together and seemed like one long day. It wasn't possible to tell when one was always alone.

People helped mark time, and Kit tried to keep track. For now, though, her focus wasn't on how much time had passed. Her thoughts were consuming the food that was on the plate in front of her. Roasted corn and beans were nothing like the ones she ate back home, but the flavors burst on her tongue in new ways. New flavors. Her stomach began to settle and feel sated. The food gave her strength.

Looking around, the doc took in a mouthful of tack bread soaked in the juice of the brisket and beans. She swallowed. "Seems like you wouldn't get much business all the way out here. Why aren't you in town?"

"Platt's Gulch? We go there some days. Not so much right now. But the cable-layers are out here today and probably for the rest of the month, and they get hungry. Plus—they got barter, got gold. They get paid good for hard work. You gonna lay cable out here?"

Kathryn had a mouthful of corn and swallowed it, then drank down half her glass as she shook her head. "No.

I'm a doctor. I wouldn't know how to lay cable if my life depended on it."

Yaja filled the rest of her glass with watered whiskey. "They need you, you know. Up there in Platt's Gulch."

"Yeah, so I heard."

The older woman said nothing to that and went back to turning and covering her brisket.

A man on a horse came over the hill while Kathryn finished up her meal, and Yaja gave her a second plate, filled with the same heaping helpings as the first. Kit smiled.

"Didn't expect you to fill it up so much a second time around. Thanks, Yaja."

"Welcome to it, Doctor Kit. You know, if you have time, would you come to my house, check on my grandkids? Make sure they're healthy?" Yaja looked at her directly, ignoring the horse and man drawing close.

Kathryn kept a wary eye on him as she answered. "I will. How old are they?"

"Thirteen and twelve. Almost grown." Yaja puffed out her chest a little, then turned back to her cooking. "T'oj is coming. That's my life-mate."

"That works for me," the doctor said between mouthfuls of brisket. She eyed the incoming man from behind her shade-spectacles, turning her face downward to her food so it wasn't obvious that she was watching.

The man dismounted his pinto and led her to the trough by the wagon. She nickered, as if complaining about something, and bent her head to drink.

"This is Kathryn Judge—she's a doctor, come to help Platt's Gulch," Yaja said. T'oj bent his head slightly and put his hand over his heart. Kit stood and returned the gesture, then sat back down when T'oj held up his hands.

"Another half-day or a day's walk from here, less from M'aqual territory." Kit said. "You two are from the M.T., yes?"

Yaja nodded as T'oj went to flag down the cable-layers for their midday meal. "Yes. This is your first time to the territory. We'd know you. You're too tall to forget."

Kathryn laughed at that—a foreign sound to her own ears. "I suppose I am."

Once Kit finished her plate and glasses, she stood to help pick up the afters that the cable-layers left behind on their way back to work. Yaja counted the trade and money, and T'oj put the cooking utensils and other pieces back into the wagon.

"So you come to stay, look after the grandkids," T'oj said as Kathryn put the plates into a wood crate with others that Yaja placed there earlier.

"I'll come give them a physical, of course," she said. She took off her shade-spectacles and regarded T'oj for a moment. He gave her a soft smile.

"The kids don't leave the territory too often but they're not interested in trading. Mi'la wants to be a teacher, and Peese wants to build. They have big ideas for the community." T'oj drained what little water was left in the trough and collapsed it, then Kit helped him heft it into the wagon.

"They sound like good people," Kathryn said. The locket felt like it gained about ten pounds and burned her chest.

"They know their community. You look young. Were you alive during the Great Strife?"

Kit nodded and put her hand on the edge of the wagon. "I was born in the middle of it. My father and mother were physicians. They took care of the ones who made it home."

Yaja helped take down the awning. Kathryn closed up the cart.

"The kids, they've never known the war, but they know all the stories and it's become part of them." Yaja looked up at Kathryn. "Seems like you know the stories, too. They're part of you."

Kit swallowed and said nothing. The horse nickered as T'oj hooked her up to the wagon, and the pair took off for M'aqual Territory with Kit sitting in the back of the wagon, feet throbbing, watching the sun begin its downward climb.

In the distance, a black horse ran wild, and for a moment, Kit thought the horse was running towards her, but it broke stride and headed in the opposite direction.

***

"The children look healthy," Kathryn said as she sat down outside. T'oj and Yaja were already seated, and their upturned, eager faces were young looking in the dying light. A campfire circle sat in the middle of the three, and T'oj built up a neat bundle of kindling to get it started.

"You were gone a long time," Yaja said. She was smiling again and Kit pulled out two skinned rabbits from her satchel.

"After I checked on the grandkids, I thought I'd get us supper," she held up the neatly skinned hares. "I have the pelts in my satchel, too, if you'd like them. My gratitude for your hospitality today."

T'oj gave a big belly laugh. "Doctor Kit, you paid for that hospitality. Paid too much."

Kit shook her head. "I know. It was worth it, though. Plus you gave me a sound place to sleep and good buffalo."

Yaja put her thumb to the side of her own face and traced it from her cheek to chin. "Thank you. But for all this, I'm giving you your dollar back."

As Yaja went into the house to get the dollar, T'oj leaned forward and spoke in a conspiratorial whisper. "She wasn't going to take your dollar in the first place. I don't think so."

"Why do you say that?" Kit put the cleaned rabbits on skewers as T'oj struck the flint and started the fire.

"She tests the newcomers from the East. If they barter too hard, too easy, or what they think is a fair trade, you know, that kind of thing. She wants to know if they're good people, and she gets a—well, it's hard to explain but in M'aqual, it's called 't'inooq'—you know t'inooq?"

Kit looked up from the rabbits and frowned. "I don't."

T'oj shrugged. "You're honest. When you don't know, you say you don't. That's a good trait." He shifted onto the ground from his low seat and grew the fire. "T'inooq is a feeling from people, like when you walk into a place and feel eyes watching you. But it's more than that. It's a knowledge you feel inside from others. Yes?"

"Yes. Yes, I think I know t'inooq. I know science, but I've had that feeling many times." Kit bit her lower lip, and went back to the rabbits, setting up a rotisserie spit over the fire. That wasn't exactly a lie.

"Well, Yaja has a fine-tuned sense for it. The first things a person says gives her a sense of t'inooq and it grows from there. She says even though you're closed up with secrets, you're full of goodness."

Kit fumbled with the spit for a moment and managed to catch the side of the spit's fork just before it fell flat. She set it back up and once the fire was hot enough, turned the rabbits over onto the rotisserie.

"You're a good hunter, too," T'oj said, then grinned playfully at her.

"After walking from Charles Town, you bet I am. I don't bag a rabbit now and then means I don't get to eat." She turned the rabbits again and then let T'oj take the spit.

Yaja returned and sat down, handing Kathryn a pouch and her dollar. "Some tobacco and papers, plus your money."

Kit held up a hand, eyes wide. "I can't accept that, Yaja. That's greedy."

But Yaja pushed the pouch into the doctor's hand until she gripped it. "Yes, you can. You take it. Enjoy it. Payment for looking after the grandkids."

With a sigh, Kit accepted the payment and put it in her satchel, extracting the rabbit pelts from a separate leather pouch inside. "They dried a little bit from earlier, but they need to lie flat, I'm sure."

She took the pouch and turned it inside out, letting it breathe so it wouldn't begin to reek of death. Yaja took the pelts from the doctor and admired them. "You make a clean cut—lots of practice."

Kit shrugged. "Surgery gave me a steady hand, and skinning is easier with practice." She eyed the pouch. "I may have to throw that away, though. You have any use for it?"

Yaja laughed and nodded. "Chew for the dogs," she said, taking the pouch to her canine. The dog stood and gripped the treat in his mouth, chewing it and shaking his head. Kit watched him a moment, small smile tugging at the corners of her mouth.

The three sat in silence as the rabbits cooked on the spit. The sun dipped below the mountains, leaving a fire-glow that lit up the sky in pink and gold. Doctor Judge took to rolling three cigarettes, the scent of sweet and spicy tobacco filling the air alongside the scents of meat cooking.

"You said you were from Charles Town, Sky Eyes?" Yaja asked.

Kit looked up as she sealed the second cigarette. "Sky Eyes? You think so?"

"Bright as the sky at noon," Yaja said. T'oj nodded and grunted an agreement.

"Thank you, I think."

Yaja and T'oj laughed again. "Just an observation—same color as one of my sons."

Kit went back to rolling the cigarettes. Yaja filled a pan with squash and beans, using the drippings from the rabbits to coat the pan.

"You danced away from the question like a butterfly from flower to flower," Yaja said. "But I didn't forget to bring my net. So, you're from Charles Town?"

Kathryn smiled. "You caught me up, Yaja. Yes. I wasn't born there—my parents were from Albion, but a family friend settled in Charles Town and the trade was so good, they invited my parents for a visit when I was only a few months old. Once they saw it, they fell in love, and we settled in there."

Kit's throat was dry. She coughed to clear it and Yaja left the pan for a moment to bring back bottles of mead. "Got these from the Trulson Traders. Good folk. I have a daughter lives in Lappland—she was like your parents. Found the place on business, studying medicine, and just never left."

The bottles opened and mead served, Yaja looked over at the doctor again. "So what brings you to the Southwest Territory?"

Kit passed out the cigarettes for after supper, keeping silent for a moment. "I heard Platt's Gulch needed a doctor, so I set out here."

"On foot," Yaja pointed with her chin toward the pinto. "No horse."

"No horse. I walked."

"That's a long walk."

The doctor shrugged. "Almost 2100 miles now."

"How long have you been walking, Doc?" T'oj took the cigarette and put it in a small pouch on his belt, giving her a smile of thanks.

Kit looked around a moment, listening to the sounds of a coyote in the distance, calling for its pack or a mate, and the songs of nightingales. "Six weeks, give or take a few days. Around that. Stop for rest, illness, or to treat someone ill along the way."

They all fell silent for a long time and listened to the sounds of Twist River nearby. Travelers before her spoke of the M'aqual being known for long stretches of silence, and Kit didn't mind. Most people spoke too much, anyway. The breaks of quiet refreshed her and renewed her mind.

"No train, not even a horse once?" T'oj checked on the rabbits but looked over at the doctor.

"No."

T'oj started to ask her another question, his face open with surprise and curiosity. Yaja held up her hand. "T'oj, nih-nih."

T'oj looked chastised and resumed cooking the rabbits.

"What does 'nih-nih' mean? Though I suppose I could guess." Kit rolled another cigarette as Yaja stirred the vegetables in the pan.

"It just means 'enough,'" Yaja said. "Platt's Gulch needed you and you came. Doesn't matter how you got here, and it doesn't matter that they weren't sick before you started your journey. That's your t'inooq, and that's yours alone."

The corners of Kathryn's mouth twitched upward. Had Yaja not been looking, she would've missed it. "T'inooq is unique to the individual, then," the doctor said after a moment. "It's like clairvoyance and whatnot?"

Yaja nodded. "It's the phenomena. All of it. Some t'inooq sees the future, some the past, some get sharp instincts. But you doubt?"

She shook her head. “No. I said to T’oj, earlier, that I feel it. Just because I’m a doctor and a scientist doesn’t mean these things aren’t scientific. They don’t break the laws of physics, and they exist. They just haven’t been studied extensively. There are charlatans who claim they have t’inooq, but they don’t. They prey on those who have lost loved ones or are needy for love and affection. It needs to be studied more, to separate the phonies from the honest ones.”

“You’re no charlatan,” Yaja said. T’oj nodded in agreement. “We always know them. They’re the ones selling their t’inooq.”

The couple smiled at her. She nodded.

Kit turned the rabbits on the spit, then left the job to T’oj as she went back to rolling cigarettes.

A rush of whispers came to Kathryn’s ears again—whispered pleas for help, a jumble of voices. She felt the headache start and tried to think about anything else. Grabbing her bottle of mead, she drank it down till the whispers ceased. Without a word, Yaja handed her another bottle with her supper.

***

With the dying light of the fire and its final fizzes and snaps, Kathryn saved her cigarettes for later while Yaja and T'oj smoked. The hot cherries glowed bright against the black backdrop of the world around them, and the smell of the sweet, spicy smoke made Kit take in deep breaths.

"You can sleep inside," Yaja said. "No need to bed down with the dogs."

Kathryn looked up from staring at her boots and the swollen feet inside them. She couldn't see them, but she could feel them, and they were screaming to her that she'd walked too long that day, and now she'd pay for it.

"I like dogs," she said. "They're good for warmth."

"Inside," T'oj said, waving a hand to the door. His eyelids were heavy from too much mead.

"Only if you insist," Kit stretched as she rose off the ground and hobbled to the house made of hard clay. She brushed aside the curtain and Yaja came in behind her. The doctor ducked in the doorway, a narrow gap between her hat and the door head.

"You're even taller indoors," Yaja said, then laughed. "Over six-feet in your boots, must be."

Having to stoop to stand under the low ceiling wasn't terrible—at least is was better than sleeping outdoors and winding up with rattlesnakes cuddling with her for warmth in the morning. "Six-foot, four inches in these," Kit shrugged a little and removed her duster, then her hat. "Thank you again."

"You're welcome, Doc. You can have the big bed. T'oj and I are smaller. We can fit on the trundle cot."

Kit bit her lower lip to suppress a laugh. It seemed like Yaja's joy was contagious, if only for a moment. "I'm much obliged. Is there a place I can wash?"

"Got a washroom and a water closet. Just off to the right of the bedroom. Running water inside. The community in Platt's Gulch built it for us when we opened our borders for trade." Yaja was making busy in the kitchen, putting food together to be ready for the next day. "You go wash, and rest. Don't need a smelly doctor."

Kit thanked her with a soft chuckle and made her way into the washroom, letting out a low whistle at just how sophisticated the adobe was, even without a proper front door. It looked so simple and basic from outside, and though the ceiling clearance was low and the floors were some unfinished pine, the indoor plumbing and gas lighting was as good as anything from home. Wishful thinking, perhaps, the doctor thought as she sat down on a small bench.

The woman who seemed impossibly tall in the little house got undressed and set her gun aside, keeping her locket and vial around her neck. She slipped into the bath and washed another three weeks off of her, then cleaned her clothes and boots. Tomorrow it'd be another layer of dust and her feet would be raw and complain, but she'd think about that later. For now, she was resting back in the warm water as her feet finally cooled, sticking out of the tub and elevated in the night air.

Eyes closed, she listened to the sounds outside, hoping the whispers would stay away—just for now. She could hear the cries for help, and she would heed them. Soon. Coyotes in the distance yipped and howled, dogs answering their calls with warnings to stay away. Birds cooed night songs to her ears and crickets told her they were ready for mates. The water cooled around her. Her heartbeat slowed, and her feet, though testy, began to calm.

When she finished bathing, she let the water run out of the tub and washed it out so the gray and orange film revealed white porcelain once more. She dried her hair and moved down to her feet, taking note of her calluses, and blisters forming over the calluses. They no longer hurt. Her observation had a cool detachment, the way a scientist looks at an interesting specimen.

She set about cleaning her gun while in the washroom—a simple task with a revolver, especially the *Colt .45 M1878* she carried. Though she was careful and conscientious, cleaning the gun was a meditative task for her. It gave her a sense of purpose, of peace. The bore brush gliding through the muzzle—careful, slender fingers ensuring that the frame was kept safe from nicks and dings while cleaning—taking care to protect the crown brought order into her life. It made things simple. Soothing.

Once the gun was clean and well-oiled, but not slippery, Kit reloaded with a moon clip and put the revolver away. Her clothes still drying, she pulled out her long-shirt and donned it, bare feet slapping softly against the floor. Sounds of the night drifted and swirled around her.

Bed, cool to the touch. The doctor nestled in, slipping past a drowsing Yaja and T'oj, and pulled a sheet over herself. She took out her locket and opened it with a quiet click, softer than the sounds of the couple in the trundle bed breathing.

Inside, a boy. No more than eleven years old—not even developing the roundness of manhood in his strong chin. His square face matched Kit's, but it would have been manlier.

It would have been.

Tears wet the edges of her eyes, making them sting, leaving a lasting burn.

Kathryn whispered three words as she clutched the picture of the boy to her heart.

"I'm sorry, son."

Sleep came in a heavy blanket over her, and the echoes of the vial clinking against the locket chased her into the darkness. The locket and vial turned into a syringe, card tricks and escape tricks—a boy's laughter, followed by the void.

***

The first streams of sunlight struck the room, and Kit pushed herself into a sitting position—looking around for a frantic second marked by a thudding heartbeat. The memories of last night came back to her—of dinner with Yaja and T'oj, of showing the grandchildren card tricks to distract them from her instruments, and falling asleep in a warm, comfortable bed. She stretched her neck from side to side and rolled her shoulders. Chatty-birds, the long-bodied blackbirds, cawed hellos to each other.

Night had provided Kit with a blackout—a deep sleep with no recall of dreams. She swung her legs to the side and they hit the cool, bare floor. The doctor was careful not to hit her head against the low ceiling.

Her feet threatened rebellion as she shook out her boots to check for scorpions and snakes that might have nestled in for the night. Neither foot held any interest in being encased in the shoes again, though they were the most comfortable ones she owned. She tapped the heel of one boot, then the other. On the last one, a small scorpion came out and skittered across the floor. Kathryn picked it up by its tail, careful of the stinger, and tossed it out the window. Once assured they were clear, she pulled on her boots. She remembered to stoop a little as she slid from the bed and kept bent over as she finished dressing.

The scent of cooked meats and corn filled the air and Kit made her way into the kitchen at the entryway of the house.

"Leftover rabbit and corn. Tell me this morning, Doctor Kit—how'd you manage to kill those rabbits at the same time?"

Yaja's words didn't make sense to Kit, at first. They ran by too fast and seemed to be in another language.

T'oj handed her a clay cup. "Here. Have coffee. Yaja can wait for answers."

Kit reached out and took the cup from T'oj, shaking her head to clear the dust that settled over her mind during the night. After a few sips, the question Yaja asked clicked into place.

"Double-action revolver and a lot of practice. I might not look like it, but I like to eat a lot, and out there, alone, there was nothing to do but hunt for my own food and follow the rivers or get water from the cacti." She drank more of the coffee and chewed up the grounds, then put the cup down. T'oj refilled it and Yaja handed her a plate. Kit thanked her.

"You shot one in the eye, and that means you've got good aim—that's a lifetime of practice, not just weeks."

Kit said nothing in return to the compliment and observation, just muttered another thanks for the food and coffee. She ate in silence, letting herself awaken. Yaja shrugged but didn't press her for answers.

Outside, faint hoofbeats grew louder with each passing second. The doctor looked toward the front of the house, and T'oj followed her gaze. The front door was open to let in the morning breeze, and a M'aqual man climbed down from his horse and stood outside. He was slightly taller than T'oj, and much younger. He had a number of tattoos running up his neck and down his arms, all lines and dots that looked to Kit like a language.

"Mish," he held up one hand, then patted his chest.

"Mish-mish," T'oj said, waving him in and motioning for him to sit. "Come inside, Waya."

Waya paused for a moment as he regarded the tall, strange woman who was looking at him with a curious expression. He held up his hand and bowed his head.

She did the same. "Kathryn Judge. I'm a guest of Yaja and T'oj's," she said.

They exchanged pleasantries in the form of nods. Yaja offered him a plate, but Waya shook his head. "Ate too much last night at Kika's," he said with what was almost a smile, then turned to the stranger. "That's my life-mate—well, soon-to-be life mate."

Kathryn went back to her meal, appearing not to be concerned with the conversation.

"Kika's going to make you too fat to ride that horse," Yaja chuckled as she spoke. T'oj grunted and mimed a horse struggling under a great weight.

"It's true, I need to be careful. But before I go down a winding trail, I'm here to ask around on business for Platt's Gulch," Waya said, looking from T'oj and Yaja to Kit. "They need a doctor, and they need one bad. I mean bad."

Kit stopped eating and looked up. "I'm a doctor. What's happened?"

"More people are getting sick," Waya said. He sat down next to the doctor and scooted his chair to lean in close. "More dying. No one knows why. They just complain of stomach upset, then head pain, and then the next thing they're sweating, shaking, and blood comes out of their eyes and noses, and they cough it up. Then they just die."

Kathryn nodded while T'oj and Yaja exchanged looks of upset and alarm—apparently they knew it was bad, but not just how bad. But the doctor wore a placid expression, taking in the information. She went back to her breakfast. "When did it start?"

"Three weeks ago, people got the pains, but now it seems to be speeding up—like they die faster now." Waya ran a hand through his hair and shivered. "You can come back with me, Doc."

The doctor finished her plate, then stood to clear it. "I don't ride horses. You go ahead. Tell them I'll be there by noon. There's something I need to do, first."

Waya left and Kit turned to Yaja. "I need to find prickle paddles. They're related to prickly pears, but they're purple with yellow tips. You know where I could find them?"

Yaja and T'oj laughed again, then Yaja slapped her own leg. "All over M'aqual Territory, that's where. Just go outside to the old well. There's a nest of them. You couldn't see them from the house, though. What'choo need 'em for?"

"Making medicine," Kathryn said. "Don't you have a doctor here? Or a chemist?"

T'oj nodded. "We do. He tried to help at Platt's Gulch but there's too many people. With our community having a cholera outbreak, it was just too much. He's sick now but that's exhaustion. Took some time to clean up the wells causing the outbreak."

"They're clean now, though, yes?" Kit looked at her coffee and refrained from grimacing.

T'oj chuckled. "Yes. Don't worry, we wouldn't bring you back here to make you sick."

"I'm sure you wouldn't." Kit gave T'oj a grim look and headed outside to the old well. It was far enough away that she couldn't see them around the back of the house, but when she got there, she understood the joke. Prickle paddle plants crammed in tight, surrounding cacti and leaving only narrow paths to navigate between them. Kit could start her own factory manufacturing medicines—they seemed to go on for acres.

The well was capped, cut down to look like an old tree stump. The doctor snorted a laugh and shook her head.

Taking a pruning knife from her satchel, she removed a small leather pouch for collection and removed the sharp tines from the paddles, small droplets of purple juice forming the way tears well in the eye when the wind blows too hard. The doctor waited for them not to weep, and when the sap hardened, she picked each paddle and put it in the pouch. She did this till she had to struggle to shut the bag. When she looked at what was left, it didn't seem like she'd done any harvesting at all.

A shadow grew behind her, but Kathryn didn't startle. She could smell the familiar scent of leather saddle and man sweat.

"You rode in the wagon yesterday," T'oj said. "But you say you don't ride horses."

Kathryn tipped her hat upward and looked at the older man, squinting against the sun behind him. She needed her shade-spectacles already. "I don't ride horses. I rode in the wagon as an exception because I couldn't keep up with you on your way home, and it would've been rude to make you wait. After the hospitality you showed me, I couldn't refuse the ride."

"That's fair." T'oj put his hands in his pockets. "You seem like a fair person."

"Hm. Is your t'inooq telling you something?" Kit stood up and put her satchel back together.

"A little. Why don't you ride horses?" T'oj asked. "I know it's not my business, but thought I'd ask."

Kit shook her head. “Used to ride. I won’t now. Not going to burden them with any bad t’inooq.”

T’oj nodded. “You understand t’inooq.”

The doctor shrugged. “Maybe a little.” She reached into her satchel once more. “Look, I know you won’t take it, but consider it an exchange to the community. For letting me take the prickle paddles. For letting me stay in your territory.”

She handed three gold nuggets to T’oj. He looked down and nodded.

“We’ll give them to the community, for when people are broke and need help.”

“Good.” Kathryn secured her satchel once more, then put her hand over her heart. “May you be prosperous.”

“May your travels be fruitful.” T’oj gave Kit a smile as he returned the gesture. “Till we meet again, Doctor Judge.”

Kit smiled back this time, but her eyes still showed T’oj hints of sadness. “Till we meet again.”

T’oj watched the doctor leave, bound for Platt’s Gulch, till she was a small silhouette at a distant point. He sighed.

"Your t'inooq isn't bad, Doctor, just out of balance."

The black horse that Kit watched earlier ran towards the town in a playful, looping motion. T'oj went back inside.

***

Noon.

The sky overhead glared a faded blue against the bright sun, and below, a crowd gathered. Expectant faces watched a figure in the distance—tall, lean, with long legs and a duster billowing against the wind, one hand on the faded black hat and the other near the hip holster.

A figure that drew closer, seemed to get even taller. The ones that were left—the healthy and strong ones—stood outside and watched her approach the town's arch. It was a simple, iron arch with an awkwardly lettered sign:

WE L COME TO PLATT'S GULCH

Kit glanced at it for a moment, then to the townspeople on either side of the street. The feeling of a fishhook caught in her heart and pulled in the other direction for a moment. It was only about twenty, perhaps twenty-five people staring, but it was enough to cause the doctor to hesitate. If only for a second.

But one foot trudged on in front of the other as it had for the last 2199 miles. The wind died down as she stepped through the threshold. It seemed as if it had been timed with her stride.

There were farmers bringing in their produce trade for the day, mothers shopping with their children, and shopkeepers coming out of their stores to take a look at the stranger walking into town. The one that promised to be here come noon.

Some stood with mouths open wide, and others scowled, but most just stared. The doctor resisted the urge to put her hand on the butt of her revolver. Her temples began to throb as the whispers began again, inside her head.

Is that The Walking Doctor that Waya was talking about?

Shit, she sure is tall—

Will she really help—

Maybe we should tell her about the sky—

Wonder where she went to school—

She looks like a fat-lipped charlatan—

Wonder if I'd catch her eye—

The voices kept pushing their way in despite Kathryn looking straight ahead to the other tall man standing at the end of the main street. He wore a silver, six-point star on his chest and a worn, brown Stetson on his head. His clothes were dusty, but fresh. A woman stood with him. Shorter, but husky in a muscular way. She wore a five-point star on her chest and her clothes were almost pristine by comparison. The man held a canteen and the woman held a basket wrapped in linen.

One by one, the whispers ceased as Kathryn focused entirely on the man in front of her. Something about him soothed the voices, made them go quiet.

“Sheriff. Deputy,” the doctor acknowledged both of them, recognizing the star’s point system. Six for sheriffs, five for deputies. The same as any town, east or west.

“Welcome to Platt’s Gulch, Doctor. Waya said you’d be here but we weren’t sure if you’d make it on time. The sun in this sector of the Southwest is brutal this time of year.” The man held up his free hand, then put it to his heart. “Diribe Onyemaechi—I’m the sheriff for the Gulch, and this is my deputy, Yina Ndubuisi.”

Kit returned the gesture. "Kathryn Judge, MD. I heard the Southwest needed doctors, but Waya told me I was needed here. I hope I can be of service."

Diribe handed Kathryn the canteen and she drank from it as Yina pulled back the linen to reveal a basket of fry bread, jams, preserves, and aged cheese. "Help yourself, please. Come in, eat, set a spell and we'll tell you about the town."

Kit held up a hand. "Thank you, but I think I'd like to go see the ones who are ill and tend to them right away."

"Sure, that's what you say, but everyone knows it's science and your so-called 'logic' that's brought this darkness to our town."

That voice—a commanding, booming voice from behind her—set Kathryn's jaw tight and put tension rods down her spine. She knew a cultist when she heard one.

This was a cultist. The ones who flocked to the Northwest and Southwest Territories to escape what they considered evil. In Kathryn's opinion, he was the most dangerous man in town. Not to her, maybe, but to the townspeople who were too easily swayed and fearful of death, the thought of an afterlife where creatures of kindness tended to their every want bringing them a false comfort. Men and women like the cultist preyed upon that vulnerability and exploited every last piece of fear.

There weren't many left out on the East Coast, but the handful that were there were poison enough. The doctor preferred to keep her encounters with them brief and with seasons upon seasons between them.

She turned to see a man standing there, wearing the typical garb of an Alastor cultist: white linen suit, satin handkerchief in the pocket with a small 'A' embroidered on the turquoise background in a shiny gold thread, and white leather shoes. Practical attire in the East, but not so in the West. The red dust that kicked up so often during the plentiful sandstorms had cast a rusty hue on what would be a blinding white suit. It would be laughable to her if she didn't despise them so much.

The doctor kept her face neutral, then angled herself so she didn't have to turn her back on him. She ignored him just the same. "I think I should be off to your hospital, or infirmary."

Diribe nodded and gave the preacher a grim look, shaking his head. "That's Nico Rice. He's got a few followers but nothing you have to worry about. Prayers don't work. Either Alastor is dead or never was."

Rice scoffed and raised a finger, pointing it at Kathryn. "This doctor will bring Death to Platt's Gulch, Sheriff. Count my words—she will bring Death."

Kit pursed her lips and Rice took a step back as if expecting her to spit on him. She didn't.

She will bring Death.

"No, I think Death's already here, from what I've heard," the doctor said.

Nico opened his mouth to answer but Yina took a step forward. "Enough of the crazy talk, Rice. You finish your business and go back to your flock. Go, or it'll be another night in the tank for raising a disturbance."

For a breath, it looked as if Rice was going to protest again, but the look on Yina's face made Kit's scowl look tame. Going pale, he turned away.

His 'flock' wasn't with him—otherwise he wouldn't shrink back, Kit thought. They were only brave in packs. She'd seen that before with other cultists. Those who tried to push for laws based on their nonsense beliefs and who were laughed at back home. They came out here in their packs, happy to be left alone but not content to leave others alone.

As the preacher stalked off, Diribe turned back to the doctor. “I’m sorry he was in town today. He’s a nasty man but he never does anything illegal enough to get bounced.” He ran a hand over his brow to keep the sweat from his eyes.

“It’s forgotten already,” Kit said. She could feel a burn high inside the bridge of her nose. The voices had been too much again, and the blood was about to start its drip outward. She sniffed and pulled her bandana around her nose and mouth.

“Oh, the dust is harsh, but you’ll get used to it,” Yina said. “The cloth helps.”

The doctor nodded. “I’ll head to the hospital if you’ll show me the way.”

They led her to the hospital as the blood made its way onto Kit’s bandana. She ducked into a washroom as they entered the building and stopped the bleeding as the voices came to a crescendo in her head. Tears of effort sprang from her eyes as she squeezed them shut.

“Please.”

Her whisper, a quiet plea to the voices to stop, seemed to be enough. They faded back into silence and the doctor found herself sitting on the edge of a toilet. She pinched her nose shut harder this time and stood. Eventually, the bleeding stopped.

Kathryn stood in front of the looking glass and examined herself, making sure the blood was cleaned from her face. Once satisfied, she washed her hands, clearing off the scarlet dots on the bone china sink.

THE INFIRM

The mercury glinted in the sunlight as Swifty turned it, squinting to read the temperature. 102.2 and climbing. They needed to calm the fevers before evening hit and people died from that alone, although it might have been more merciful than what was happening to them.

"We'll get you some cool packs. Here, sit up a little and drink this water. Fresh from the spring, not from the sink." Swifty put the thermometer back in its glass casing and poured a cup of water.

The man in his early twenties—a man Swifty had known since they were both little shavers—sat up and sipped his water. It went down. The man made a gasping sound, as if taking a sip had spent all his energy.

"Now you keep that down, and rest. When you wake up, I'll give you more to drink." Swifty patted Nelson's hand and stood up, back aching as it cracked. He was too young to feel this old, but only getting two or three hours of sleep each night aged him. The other day, Swifty caught a glimpse of himself in the looking glass hanging over the infirm and saw a trail of gray hairs emerging on his right temple. He was far too young for gray hair at only twenty-five, yet there they were, sprouted like stubborn weeds in a flower garden.

Nelson laid back down after another sip of water and closed his eyes. The fever kept him shivering and Swifty pulled his blanket up to let him sweat it out. Maybe it would help, but his heart sank at the truth.

His childhood friend was going to die.

"Take that blanket off him. He'll die faster if you keep him covered."

Swifty turned to tell the owner of that voice to shut her trap but stopped and stared at the stranger. She was tall, with strong bones and smooth skin, and faded sky eyes that stood out among wisps of jet black hair he could see under her hat. Those eyes gazed at him knife-sharp, the way his mother looked at him when he spoke out of turn.

He felt his face get hot and swallowed hard, finding his voice. "I—excuse me, ma'am—you must be the doctor Waya told us about. I'm Swift Slater, but everyone calls me Swifty."

"What do you call yourself, then?" The woman raised her eyebrow at him and he felt his face grow hotter—thought he might have to lie down a moment.

"Oh, Swifty's fine. I don't mind what people call me as long as they call me now and then. Although I think they still call me Swifty because they think I'm a kid, still." He smiled and put his hand over his heart. She did the same over hers.

"Kathryn Judge. You can call me Kit if you prefer. Doc, Kit, and Kathryn are fine with me." She looked around the sick ward at the neatly lined up beds in the long, white room. "Any survivors, yet?"

"Right to work—uh—no, Doc. None. They come in when the stomach pains get bad and at first we—me and the M'aqual's doctor, I mean—thought it was just a few flares of food poisoning. They had fever, stomach aches, general malaise, and then the bleeding started."

He spoke the last in hushed tones in case Nelson was aware of what he was saying.

Kit nodded. "Who is or was your first patient?"

"She's a 'was,' I'm sad to say. Her name was Ella Greene, thirty-one, mother of seven. She came in about three weeks ago, and her husband had to carry her in by coach. He didn't get sick and his children are fine, too." Swifty's hands shook as he ran them through his hair.

At this, Kathryn raised her brows. "Still fine? Nothing?"

"I asked Diribe to check on them yesterday. Aside from Virgil and the kids being upset about losing Ella, they're fine. Physically fine."

Kit frowned. "Not contagious, perhaps."

"No, not that we've noticed. Seems to hit people at random, like a bad lottery."

She waved her hand at him in a gesture to move on. "What's the population?"

"Last census had us at 1,428, but we're not all on top of each other. Platt's Gulch has a lot of land that's surrounded by the M'aqual and Turepo Territories. They provide us a lot of protection in exchange for our goods." Swifty scratched the back of his neck. "But yes, it seems random as to who it hits."

"Protection from what?" Kathryn raised her eyebrow at him.

"All kinds of wild animals and other things. It's not all desert around here as you can see, but there are a lot of desert creatures. The Turepo and M'aqual know how to deal with them better'n we do, so we're glad to have them handy by."

The doctor took a good look around and Swifty watched her watching the patients, the room, and finally him. Her gaze was still hard to bear, but he met it and held it.

"What's your medical background?" she asked.

"New Culvert City Nursing School, class of '97. Hands shake too much for surgery, but I can hand over the instruments just fine." Swifty smiled.

Kit approximated a smile in return, just the curve of the mouth upward, not big enough to bare her teeth. "Well I'd be lost without a good nurse, and you seem like a good nurse."

Swifty beamed at that and though he'd managed to calm himself from earlier, the doctor made his face grow warm all over again. He took a deep breath. "I can only hope, Doc. But I sure do hope you don't wind up like our last doc."

"The one from M'aqual Territory? Why?"

The man shook his head. "No, not him, the one we had when this first started three weeks ago. About a week into treating then new patients, he got sick. Well, I mean before that, he went mad."

Kit folded her arms across her chest. "I'm not surprised that you're the first to tell me about this, but go on, Nurse Slater."

He brightened at being called by his title and surname. "Well, Doc Harlan was our only doctor and had been since I was a tyke. So we all knew him really well."

Kit held up her hand. "You mean to tell me with a population of over a thousand people, you only had one physician? You've pulled my hair."

"No, no hair pulling, Doc. I'm not the kind of person to tease another. Maybe I didn't explain well enough."

"Well, you do tell a story in bits and pieces—but go on," Kathryn said.

Swifty cleared his throat. "We used to have enough physicians to fill the hospital but we hit some hard times. There was a drought about two years ago that nearly turned this place into a ghost town. People moved on, and so did the physicians. The ones that stayed were steel haired and needed a cane. But when the population started booming again after the crisis passed—thanks to travelers, of course—influenza hit, and they got sick with it, and died. So—one physician standing, the rest dead, and no one here decided to take up the mantle of medicine."

Swifty started to lead the doctor to the end of the room and opened a cabinet. It was stocked with rows of bottles labelled in perfect block print. Medicines. For a variety of ailments. He took aspirin from a supply bottle and doled it into tiny paper cups.

Kit looked back around at the ill, then back to Swifty. "And your chemist?"

"Got a few of those and they supply us with medicine. We're a bit too far from the rail—you probably noticed that—but they do regular stagecoach deliveries. We're swimming in supplies. Till you came along, though, it's been me, the doc from M'aqual, and five chemists." Swifty used a clean towel to wipe sweat from his forehead. "To be genuine with you, Doc, we'd be lost without our chemists."

Kit gave a grunt of agreement. "That's usually how it works in my experience. A good chemist is a true gift. Pharmacy is a real specialty." She sighed and watched

Swifty dispense the medication into the cups. "Well, let's go on with giving them aspirin, though only enough to bring down the fever. If there's bleeding involved, aspirin will make it worse," Kit said. "325 milligrams PRN PO Q eight."

Swifty nodded. "Yes, doctor. 325 milligrams every eight ours orally as needed."

"You follow protocol. I'm glad," she said.

"Don't be too surprised, Doc. The regs were put there for a reason. I've seen what happens when nurses don't repeat back what they hear." He shuddered a bit dramatically, then turned away with the tray.

While the younger man dispensed medicine, Kit walked from bed to bed, examining the patients. When she returned, and Swifty met up with her, her face was pinched and somber, even more so than before.

"Walk with me," Kit said, heading outside the ward's doors. Swifty motioned to a young girl with a milky left eye. He told her to tend to bedpan changes while he walked with the doctor. The girl, who kept looking away from the doctor, gave a nod and scurried away.

"Kelly's a good girl, but she's a bit slow. Fell off a horse and hit her head. Coma for three days."

Kit didn't turn to look at the girl but looked at Swifty, face stern. "Does her history have medical relevance?"

Swifty looked like she'd just slapped him. "No, oh no, Doc, I just wanted you to know why she acts a bit funny, is all."

Kit waved her hand as if shooing a bug. "Irrelevant. 'Funny' is subjective and gossip is asinine. Now, before I left you to check the patients, you were going to tell me about the former doctor who was here. Tell me everything—because after what I've just witnessed, it might be medically relevant."

The nurse, who looked like a chastised child, led Kathryn to a small office with ashen walls, a simple wood desk, and three chairs. Shelves with models of organs and human bones lined the walls, interspersed with fat medical texts.

"This is usually the doctor's office," Slater said. "It's not much."

The doctor shook her head. “It doesn’t need to be. It’s functional.” Kit took the doctor’s chair behind the desk and removed her hat. Dark hair spilled out from under it. She swept it up again, tying a tight ponytail at the crown of her skull using the leather string from the hat. With a sigh, she turned her focus on the nurse. “Alright then, Slater. Don’t hold anything back.”

Nurse Slater held her gaze, then swallowed hard, shifting in his seat. “Well, I told you he was here with us, tending the sick and trying to figure out what was happening. One night, he was on his way out to ride home, and he told me he had an idea about what was making people sick. Didn’t say much else. Got on his horse and I suppose he rode home. But then he didn’t come back the next day. I called on my parents to go out to his house to look for him.”

Swifty sighed and ran his hand through his hair, again. She motioned for him to continue.

“My Papa said the horse was there, grazing, but other than that it didn’t look like the doc had ever made it home—no dishes in the sink and the bed was made. So either he left early in the morning, or didn’t get home. And why he'd leave without his horse wouldn't make sense on account he was still saddled. Mama pointed that out to us, of course. She might be blind in one eye but that other one's observant."

Kit sat forward and moved her hat to one side of the desk so she could lean. "Right. Sounds like something happened and the horse went home after losing his rider."

"Yep, and he was skittish, too, when Papa approached him, so we thought something bad happened. You know how horses are. Figured the doc got caught up in a trade dispute, maybe. That's not uncommon around here," the nurse shrugged. "Anyway, we weren't sure and for three days, we were without a doctor. More people were coming in with symptoms and kept filling up the ward."

"Three days. Then he came back, I presume."

"You got it, Doctor," Swifty said. He was frowning and it looked like his eyes were shining, but he held onto the tears. His breath shook as he spoke again. "Poor doctor. The sheriff was here, helping out with the dying as best he could. You know, dispensing medicine and keeping people comfortable. The doc came bursting in the front door. He was pale and jabbering. No one could understand him. He ran to the sheriff and clutched onto Diribe's vest, started shaking him violently. Diribe held onto him, and then the bleeding started. Came out his eyes, his nose, and bubbling out his mouth."

He put his hand up to his eyes and wiped at them. "Sorry, Doc. I just knew him a long time."

Kit reached into her pocket and pulled out a clean handkerchief. Her normally stony face softened a touch. "Here. Dry your eyes."

Swifty did, and Kit motioned for him to keep the cloth. "Thanks, Doc. Anyhow, I don't know if he caught sick looking for whatever it was and the fever made him delirious, or if something else happened. We cremated him in a town ceremony. Just about every healthy person showed up to pay their respects."

He dabbed at his eyes as he recalled the memory. "But what really bothers me are the last two words he managed to gargle out under all that blood as Diribe held him. Just two words, and then he was gone: I know."

Kit repressed a shiver. "He knew. He knew what?" she sat back and shook her head. "I don't suppose we'll find out now that he's gone."

"No, we won't. I just figured he wasn't making any sense at first, but then those words struck me later on at the service. What did he know—about the illness? Or was he just delirious?" The nurse shrugged, looking at the stranger with expectant eyes.

"Could be anything. Or nothing. I wish I had some answers for you." Kit sat back and looked around. "And speaking of answers, I have this office, but is there a pathology lab I could work in? I want to get started right away."

"Oh, yeah, of course, Doc. I'll show you around." Swifty started to rise, but Kit waved her hand at him to keep seated.

"No, just point the way and I'll see to it. In the meantime, I want you to collect specimens. Blood, urine, and stool. Do you have microscopes here?" Kit stood up and hung her hat on the coatrack, taking off her duster and rolling up her shirt sleeves.

"Yeah, we just got some—been trying to keep the place as modern as possible to attract new doctors. Looks like it worked." Swifty smiled at her.

Kit didn't return the smile, but patted Swifty's shoulder. "It worked faster than a roadrunner, Slater."

She hurried out the door in the direction the nurse showed her, face set like the mountain-scape on the horizon.

***

"The madness is, my children, that this 'doctor' with her so-called reason and science, is allowed near these suffering people," Rice said to his swaying penitents. They'd crowded into their one-room meeting hall. What they lacked in number, they made up for in belief.

They let out sighs and noises of agreement with their Hallowed Man, the one who claimed he knew the Secrets of Alastor and the Timeworn Order, Alastor's greatest enemy. Well, his greatest enemy next to science and reason. Rice's lips pulled back into a smile that resembled a snarl.

"What do we do, Hallowed One? How do we stop her? How do we save the ones who are ill?" A woman with red hair in tight corkscrew curls asked, a blush on her freckled face. Rice walked over to her and caressed her face with one unblemished-by-labor hand. She swooned.

"We keep a vigil for the wretched ones who brought this illness upon themselves," Rice said, first to the young woman and then to the crowd. "But we do nothing. Not yet. Alastor has spoken to me and says it's not time to intervene. The time will come, and the doctor will be shown the light and the way."

Rice took out his collection basket and handed it to the red-haired woman. "For now, we give our monetary sacrifices and pray for things to get better. That's the way. The only way."

Coins and money beads clattered into the collection basket as it passed from hand to hand, and Rice turned around to his pulpit, sinking to his knees. His arms stretched out, rising skyward as the collection basket filled with clinks and clatters. Away from the crowd, he grinned to himself, and this time, it was worse than a snarl. Much worse.

His eyes were full of hatred.

When he turned back to the crowd, he was full of light and care once more, taking the collection basket and setting it aside as if it weren't important. It sat next to the pulpit, leaning against the lectern in an almost haphazard fashion, as though not done on purpose.

"My children, you are pure and clean. You will not fall ill, for you are Alastor's Protected Ones. Stay with me and The Way, my children, and you will remain untouched. But stray, even once, towards the Path to Perdition, and you will be tainted forever."

The crowd whooped and made other noises that were akin to ecstasy, and Rice gave another alligator smile.

***

The pathology lab was just as modern as anything back home in Charles Town. Swifty hadn't been exaggerating about that. There were microscopes running on electricity—powerful enough to see the germs that might be what was vexing the people of Platt's Gulch.

Kit put on protective gear for her eyes, nose, and mouth, as well as protective gloves. Though it didn't seem to be contagious (families didn't get sick and didn't seem to make each other sick, plus people who had no interactions came down with the symptoms at varying times), she wasn't about to take the risk.

The answers might be under the microscope.

She set up for testing, arranging her reagents, gathering her equipment, and ensuring a clean, ready environment. The equipment gleamed with newness—though it had not been used in some time (since the hospital lost its pathologists and staff. The pristine condition indicative of long days from those left behind, keeping everything in working order.

Swifty came in after some time with 45 specimens all neatly labeled with patient's names and birthdates as well as their sexes.

"That was fast," Kit said. "You did all that alone?"

"Oh, no ma'am," Swifty shook his head. "Had some of the other volunteers help out. Sheriff came by to see if there was anything he could do, too, so I put him to work."

"Well, put yourself down for a gold star," she said, then read the downcast face of the nurse. "I mean it. That's the kind of determination that helps us sort out these messes."

That seemed to soften Swifty's mien, and he gave her a small smile. "I'm stubborn. I won't let you down."

"Normally I'd say time will tell, but your evidence so far speaks to that fact."

A blush sprouted on the young man's face, but he said nothing. As the door clicked shut behind him, the doctor got to work.

***

Diribe looked over the beds in the ward and sighed. Sicknesses came and went. This was life. "Every generation has a plague," he said as the nurse left to take the specimens to Doctor Judge. "This one happens to be ours."

"I'd pay my last coin to be able to give it back," Swifty said, balancing the tray as he walked out.

The sheriff nodded and looked around from bed to bed, listening to the coughs, waiting for one to squeeze out their last breath, and getting ready to take the swaths to them. Wrap them tight, bring them to the undertaker for burning. The same as it had been when the first doctor was trying to figure it all out, losing patient after patient.

Bodies piled up in spurts. They'd examined the water, the common gathering places people met—for Saturday Suppers or the meeting hall for dances and come up with nothing.

"Water?" A voice came from the middle of the room. Diribe strode over and poured a glass from the pitcher.

"Sit up, Carmen," Diribe helped the young woman get upright so she could drink. "Sip slow, okay?"

"Okay," her raspy voice cut itself off as she took a few sips. She made a rattling sigh. "Thanks. Who was that woman?"

"That's our new doctor." Diribe set the glass down and wiped off his hands. "Kathryn Judge."

"Judge, like an honorable judge." She nodded, eyes bright for a moment, the way they used to dance with mischief before she fell ill. A trickle of blood leaked from her left eye. "An arbiter of justice."

"That's right. She's from the east."

"Of course she is," Carmen said, taking the corner of her gown and dabbing her face with it. "That's what the whispers say."

Diribe shifted his weight from one foot to the other. "The whispers still tell you things, Carmen?"

She nodded. "They don't get sick so they hang around," she chuckled, then coughed. "I'm going to beat this, Sheriff. You just wait and see."

He looked down at her frail frame. The bleeding around her eye had stopped and he shook his head. “If anyone has the willpower to stop being sick from it, it’s you, Carmen. Did the whispers tell you if you’d live through it?”

Carmen sat back and settled her body deeper into the mattress. “They tell me I still have things to do. Can’t be doing those things if I’m dead, true?”

“True. Then maybe the doctor will have something good for us.” He leaned forward and patted Carmen’s hand. “Get some rest. You need to rest.”

“Sheriff’s orders?”

Diribe smiled. “You know it.”

Carmen closed her eyes. As her breaths became long and smooth, the sheriff let go of her hands and walked away to the wash station.

Footsteps behind him alerted Diribe to Swifty’s return. They were, like his nickname, swift and brisk. The young man always walked with purpose.

“What did she say?” he asked the nurse.

Swifty shrugged. “She’s not much of a chatty-bird,” he said. “Very businesslike. She seemed pretty impressed with the condition of the lab and the quickness of our work.”

"It doesn't take so long with extra hands," Diribe checked the clock over the door. "How long do you think this'll take?"

"As long as it takes. I'd go home and get some supper. She doesn't strike me as the type who takes long rests."

The sheriff chuckled. "No, sir. She took over like the place was hers, didn't she?"

"And that's a good sign."

"It is." Diribe paused and toweled off his hands, then threw the towel in the hamper. "Very well. I'll be back tomorrow morning. Call on me if you need."

Swifty agreed and bid him goodnight, and the sheriff strode out of the hospital.

***

Forty-five specimens later, Kathryn pulled away from the microscope. Beads of sweat covered her forehead and her throat ached from dryness. She checked her pocket watch. More time had passed than she'd realized.

Her stomach growled and she stretched, hearing and feeling bones in her spine creak and pop. She felt like an hourglass losing sand faster and faster, as if there were a hole in the bottom—it was emptying, and there wouldn't be another turn.

She pushed the grim thought from her mind and wiped sweat from her face using her shirt sleeve. There was no point in moving forward or collecting more specimens. Not right now.

What was causing this outbreak was beyond her. For the moment.

You'll find it, Kathryn. The only welcome voice in her head was the one of her father's, deep and baritone. It softened the other voices, kept them from hurting her.

The voices were often the loudest when she wasn't concentrating, allowing her mind to wander. Though the work on the disease kept her mind focused and was difficult work, the energy she devoted to it took the voices away, and her fatigue was a blissful one by comparison to when the cacophonous voices started their pleas.

Kit emerged from the pathology lab and closed the door behind her with a soft click, then made her way back to the sick ward.

"Any luck, Doc?" Swifty broke into a trot to make his way down the long hall so he could speak to her in hushed tones.

"I can't isolate a virus, or see anything unusual in their blood, urine, or stool samples," Kit said. "Whatever it is might be too small for our microscopes. I need something bigger. More powerful. Those are quite the advanced electron microscopes, but even with the dye I couldn't get anything. We don't have time for waiting on an order for something better, so I need to work backwards."

Swifty nodded. "Imagine it's something you could see."

"I suppose." Kit rubbed the back of her neck with a thin-fingered hand. "What we have is an acute, virulent, hemorrhagic fever with high morbidity, possibly one-hundred percent, but no evidence of how it transmits from one person to another. We need to check the water, for pests, for any connection that might be causing people to get sick."

"It can't be the water—wouldn't everybody get sick?" the nurse pursed his lips and knit his brows.

"Not necessarily. There's more than one source of water, even around here. We need to find what sources they're using and test them. Find all the common threads, even if they seem unlikely." She paused. "Do you read Sherlock Holmes?" Kit's expression was serious and Swifty imitated it. Though not intentional, it was a fair mimic.

"Only a couple of stories. Mostly I spend time reading my medical journals and a few personal subscriptions. So you're our Holmes?"

"If you're my Watson, Slater," Kit did grin a little that time, and Swifty brightened.

"I'm your Watson, Doc."

The tiny grin turned into a gentle smile, but it didn't last long. Kit's face went back to its usual impassive seriousness. "Well what seems trivial to some wasn't trivial to him. Often it allowed him to stay ahead and deduce things that others couldn't even perceive," she said. "The first thing we need to do is start gathering volunteers and showing them how to take clean samples—of water, bedding, and that. At the same time we need to get people to survey the households. Ask them what they were doing before they got sick. Get the stories, look for common threads. Anything. A river where they all wash. A stray dog they all feed. A mouse in every corner. Things like that, and—"

"Doctor, nurse, hurry, it's Mister Jackson. Mister Jackson," Kelly came running towards the two and pointing to a man sitting up, coughing blood. He was trying to get out of bed and runners of red slime ran down the front of his hospital gown.

Kit and Swifty rushed towards Mister Jackson, Swifty grabbing a bedpan to catch the blood vomitus, and Kit moving in to check his vitals. "Pulse is thready and tachy." She listened with her stethoscope but pulled away quickly as Jackson turned blue and fell backward.

"Pneumothorax. How long was he coughing?" Swifty prepped a tube and scalpel and handed it over to the doctor. Kelly started to cry.

"I don't know. Ten minutes, maybe longer. Oh please don't hurt him. Don't cut him open."

"Turn around and look away, Kelly," Kit said. "You don't want to see this."

But the girl didn't turn away. Instead, she collapsed on the floor and began rocking back and forth, babbling. Two nurse's aides rushed to Swifty's side.

"Get Kelly out of here, now," the doctor said to the aides while she slid a tube between Jackson's ribs. "Swift, hold the patient firm."

With the intubation finished, Jackson's face stopped turning blue, although it was as white as chalk. Swifty gave her the patient's vitals and Kit shook her head.

"He's lost too much blood. He needs a transfusion. Do we have a blood bank?"

"We do, Doc," Swifty said. He was shaking from the effort of holding Jackson down, wiping his hands on the rags used for clean-up.

Kit sighed. "Give him five units."

"Doc, I don't think—"

"Five units."

But Jackson made a gurgling noise and motioned her closer with a thick-fingered hand. Kit leaned in so she could hear him talk.

"What is it, Mister Jackson?"

"The sky. Check the sky."

He closed his eyes, and his breath stopped.

Kit felt for a pulse, jaw set, temples pulsing. Her eyes roved over him, willing him to come back to life and tell her what the hell he meant.

She pulled back and left the room, letting herself into the washroom with sticky, bloody hands. If only she could *hear* them all the time, she'd understand.

The doctor washed her hands until they were raw.

A knock at the door interrupted her, and Kit dried her face with a towel, then opened the door. "What?"

"Just seeing if you're okay, Doc—you were gone awhile and it's suppertime. Not many of the sick feel like eating, but the aides are seeing to them. Kelly calmed down after a while, so I made her go home." Swifty ran a hand through his hair. "You want some chili and corn bread? The saloon's going to house you—it's not far from here, and they've got the best chili."

"I could eat. Have Mister Jackson prepped for an autopsy, and we'll go to the saloon for a quick dinner. How many patients do we have now?"

"With Mister Jackson gone? Thirty-three. The aides can tend to them, Doc. There's nothing we can do for them right now, and you've got to eat." Swifty sounded like a fretful old woman.

The doctor reached for a tin of skin balm and rubbed it on her hands. "It's fine, Slater. You're my Watson, not my mother. I know I'm not going to work well if I don't have fuel for my brain. Tell whomever you need to prep Jackson, and then we'll head out for an evening meal."

"Yes, ma'am. I'll have the aides move him to the morgue. Some of the volunteers can stay with the patients. And Doc?" Swifty looked at her with huge eyes.

"What is it?" She tipped her head at him.

"You can't save them all."

The doctor shook her head and said nothing, pushing past Swifty as she exited the washroom. As she picked up her belongings from her office, she headed for the front door. The nurse wasn't far behind.

I couldn't even save one.

***

Pig-Nose Polly ran a good saloon and boarder house, Swifty told Kit as they walked in together. He introduced Kit to the round-faced blonde with the upturned nose. She wasn't just round in the face, but curved in many places, and Kit's eye wandered over those curves.

"It'll be good for business to have a new Doc in town. Help keep my charges clean, and maybe the food, too." Polly grinned at Kit as she put her hand to her heart. She leaned in close. "You ever need a night to let off steam with one of my guys or gals, I'll make sure they treat you right."

Swifty was too busy tucking into his chili and cornbread, or at least he looked that way when Polly was talking. Kit sat with the dish in front of her but turned her head up to the blonde's.

"If I'm ever looking to let off steam, I'll look for *you*."

Polly gave a good laugh and handed Kit an extra helping of cornbread, then poured out glasses of whiskey for the two of them. "We've got ale, mead, and plenty of other spirits to delight you, Doc. Say the word and it's yours. Just glad to have you here."

When the woman excused herself, Swifty gave Kathryn a sheepish smile. "She really likes you, not just because you're a doc, either. I think she misses her Betty Sue."

"One of her girls?" Kit raised one eyebrow. "Is this medically relevant, or more gossip?"

"It's *mentally* relevant, Doc. I took you serious when you said you didn't gossip." Swifty dipped a corner of the cornbread into the chili and ate it before speaking again. "Betty Sue was her wife. They were together for a long time, at least since they moved here, maybe before." He shrugged.

Kit shook her head. "I don't see how it's mentally relevant." She narrowed her eyes at Swifty. "Did she die of the disease?

"No, she died long before that."

The doctor shrugged. "Oh, fine then. I suppose I know why you're telling me this. You want me to be careful for her fragile grief state."

Swifty nodded. "And I think I know you're going to tell me to mind my own business."

"No, now I'm not. You did it for me."

Taking a spoonful of the chili, she prepared herself for the heat she knew it would have. Though Charles Town had hot peppers and chilies that burned holes in her tongue, it seemed mild in comparison with the food she'd tasted out west. She'd grown accustomed to it, but the first time she ate it, it stopped her trip to Platt's Gulch for two days.

The first bite sent alarms ringing down her tongue and fires started in her ears. Kit's eyes stung and watered, and her eyebrows threatened to pop off in pools of sweat. She kept eating. The burn felt like being cleansed by fire. Even her ears tingled. Her neck followed suit. Passionate kisses of heat rose from the inside. She followed it with whiskey, and at that point, the burn of the alcohol didn't matter, it didn't touch the heat from the chilies. In fact, it cut the oil down and helped reduce the burn.

A bite of the soft, crumbling cornbread quenched the fire, and Polly came back over with two bowls full of fruit mixed with a sweet cream. "We've got some fruit salad to cool you down, Doc, and I have water if you need it."

"I'll take the fruit. I'm fine without the water, although if you have coffee, I'll take some of that." Kit's voice was hoarse as Polly put the bowl in front of her. "You make a hot, fine chili, Polly. I've never seen it with ground meat and cut chunks together before, but I'm from back east."

The woman with the upturned nose laughed and slapped the doctor's arm. "Well that's all bison and demon peppers, really. I do put a few other spices in and a secret ingredient, and if you guess what it is, I'll give you ten dollars."

Kit put another bite in her mouth and let it heat up again, rolling it over her tongue, tasting something with a slight bitterness to it, and a familiar, almost sweet taste. She motioned Polly to lean down so she could whisper in the woman's ear. "It's chocolate."

Polly pulled back as if Kathryn had performed a feat of magic. "I owe you ten dollars. That's a talented tongue you have, Doc."

"That's just the start," Kit said, then winked at Polly. She went back to her food as if she hadn't said a word and picked some fruit from the bowl to cool off her palate.

"Got any other tricks up your sleeve?" Polly asked.

Kit winked. "I just might."

A flustered blush rose to Polly's face and she tried to make herself busy clearing utensils off the table. She stumbled, and a knife went sailing towards the floor.

In a flash, Kit whipped her hand out and caught it mid-air by its handle. She twirled it in her hand, offering to Polly.

"Clever hands, too," Polly said.

"So I've been told." She pulled a ten-dollar bill out of thin air. "This the tenner you owe me?"

Polly's jaw dropped as she felt her pockets. "How on earth did you do that?"

"I'm sworn to secrecy," Kit said.

Once Polly was gone again, Kit looked back to Swifty. "So Betty Sue is no longer with us, and what else are you trying to tell me?"

Swifty kept eating, seeming unbothered by the heat of the chili. "She died three years ago in a shoot-out. Polly wasn't the same for a long time, and I've never seen her smile so big since. Till you got here. Now the smile—well, it's in her eyes."

Kit nodded. "I'll keep that in mind. Wouldn't want to be a heartbreaker."

Swifty shook his head. "I don't think you can help that, Doc."

"I was pulling your hair, Slater."

"Oh—oh it was a joke. That's a good one, Doc," Swifty chuckled and shook his head. "I'm sorry, Doc. I just haven't been able to joke around since all this started."

Kathryn shrugged. “I’m not all that good with jokes, myself. I usually don’t entertain much. I’m just here to heal. Sometimes people need to laugh, though.”

“You don’t laugh much, Doc. You’re real serious all the time.” Swifty traded his chili bowl for the fruit bowl. “I didn’t realize you’d even made a joke because of it; you know?”

Her face was solemn. “There’s not much for me to laugh about, but everyone needs a break now and then.”

“That’s the core truth, Doc.” Swifty changed out his fruit for more chili. “You get used to the heat of the demon peppers.”

“Hottest I’ve ever had. They don’t get this hot at home, but you’re right, I’ll get used to it.”

They finished their meal in silence, and Polly brought over some coffee.

“There’s a room upstairs that’s all yours, Doc, and no charge, of course. Your room and board, and all your food and drinks are on the house as long as you stay to work. The gals and guys are all yours, too.”

Kit shook her head. “I’m sorry, Polly, but I’ll have to decline the offer of people. They’re their own, not mine.”

Polly's smile faltered a bit and a look of confusion crossed her face. "Oh, I mean their services of course."

"Of course." Kit turned to her coffee as Polly left again.

"You know, Doc, if you're interested I don't think it'd hurt," Swifty said as he swallowed the bitter, black drink.

"I'm not interested."

"You don't think she's attractive?"

"Didn't say that." Kit drank her own hot drink down by half and put it on the table with a soft clatter. "Polly's lovely."

"Yeah, she is, and she's real kind."

"I agree—very jovial as well."

After coffee, Kit stood up and left two quarters on the table. "Back to the hospital. We've got an autopsy to perform."

***

"The patient is a man identified as Jorge Manuel Santiago Jackson, age sixty-seven, and in apparent good health prior to the recent outbreak. According to his medical records, the patient suffered from mild osteoarthritis, and occasional headaches. Otherwise no medical conditions found."

Kit spoke into a slender phonograph cylinder as she stood over the body of Jackson. Swifty stood on the other side of the slab, holding a camera on a tripod, pointed at the body to take pictures of their discoveries.

"The deceased is five-foot-ten and one-hundred-fifty-five pounds. His apparent age was older than his stated age, characterized by extensive rhytids at the perioral and sub-ocular regions." Kit stopped recording for a moment and put on her paper mask over her lips and nose, then put on her goggles. Swifty stopped fiddling with the camera and did the same.

The doctor adjusted her gloves, then resumed recording. "The deceased is survived by one daughter, Margarita Snow Santiago Jackson-Nadeau. She identified the deceased positively as her father."

She turned to the body but continued speaking. "Visual inspection of the body reveals no lesions or inconsistencies with a natural death. Puncture wounds along the arm are consistent with intravenous administration of fluids and blood. The body was stripped for autopsy and the remains of one hospital gown soaked in blood from the deceased's vomitus has been discarded to the incinerator after inspection by this physician. There were no unusual fibers or traces of any other substance."

After that, Kit made a Y-incision along the body, and Swifty poised himself to take the first picture of what they would find inside. When the doctor opened up the chest cavity, she stopped recording for a moment, eyebrows raised. "What the hell is this?"

Swifty shook his head and shrugged, face losing what color it had left. Kit took a step back so that he could take the photograph without her hands in it.

Kathryn used her foot to trigger the sound recorder once more. "Visual inspection of the patient's chest cavity reveals the lungs are—or appear to be—in a gelatinous state. While the alveoli, bronchial tubes, and outer edges of the lungs appear intact, the majority of the organ appears to have turned into a jelly-like substance."

She continued her inspection of the rest of the body, reaching in to remove the heart. It made a small sucking sound in her hand, then collapsed into more gelatinous material and seeped through her fingers. "I can't even get a scalpel in to remove it, and now it appears the heart was turned into a gelatinous material as well."

Swifty kept snapping pictures as the autopsy continued.

Kit reached down to cut open the stomach. “The stomach, liver, spleen, intestines, and kidneys appear to be intact. Stomach contents include blood, prickly pear slices which are mostly undigested, and white rice, which is partially digested. There is little of it, which coincides with the nurse’s report that he was suffering from a lack of appetite.” She shook her head. “Contents are consistent with midday meal served today by the nurse’s aides.”

She glanced at Swifty, then back down at the body. “Removing samples of each to take to the pathology lab for further analysis. Moving on to the brain.”

Swifty took a few more pictures. When he was finished, he moved the samples that Kit took over to the worktable and prepped them while the doctor took out the bone saw to slice into Jackson’s skull.

“The brain is intact, weighing one-thousand three-hundred sixty-eight grams, showing no signs of atrophy, lesions, or hemorrhage.” The doctor made careful, thin slices of the brain meat, setting it in petri dishes. “Sending samples for further examination in pathology.”

She sighed and continued her work. “I’m going to have to take a cross-section of the brain for more information.”

When she sliced into the center of the brain and examined it, her eyes widened. "What is *this*?"

Swifty angled the camera to take pictures of the cross-section of brain matter in her hand. "Jackson's brain appears to have some kind of black, speckled matter inside of it. It appears as if his brain has tiny pinpoints that would make it appear spongiform, but the matter comes off on the fingers when rubbed." Her eyes sought Swifty's. "Good thing we're wearing gloves."

Popping the matter into a collection tube, Kit put the rest of Jackson back together and finished the autopsy.

She stopped recording. "Slater, how about you close Mister Jackson up, and I'll scrub out then take these samples over to path?"

"Sure thing, Doc. But this is—I don't know. This is strange."

"What's that?" Kit tossed her gloves in the incinerator and her mask followed.

"Doctor Harlan did an autopsy but didn't find anything like this. At least I don't think he did." Swifty grimaced.

"What do you mean 'you don't think' the doctor found anything like this?" Kit put her hands on her hips and studied Swifty with hard eyes.

"He did the autopsy by himself, Doc, and never told anyone what he found. He just rode off—and that was when he died. Plus, no one can find his autopsy notes. I think they were stolen but there's no evidence that he even took any in the first place." Swifty shifted from one foot to the other.

Kit shook her head and put one clean hand on the back of her neck, giving it a squeeze. "Why didn't you tell me this before?"

"I didn't really think about it before, Doc. Until you did the autopsy today I just didn't give it a kitten's whisker."

"I suppose you've been overwhelmed." She shrugged and collected her samples. "Well, it doesn't really matter for now. But it's something that Diribe should look into, I would think—about potentially stolen documents. You should call on him in the morning to have him investigate."

Swifty put his disposables in the incinerator and brought Kathryn the trolley. "Here, Doc. And I will. You think we'll figure this out, though?"

Kit frowned. "If we stick to logic, reason, and scientific investigation, we will—or our successors will."

***

"Disappointment and fatigue was the only thing I got out of this night," Kit took a shot of whiskey and followed it with a drink of half her beer. "I could be onto something. Slater and I spent half the night running between samples and taking care of people slowly dying of—a hemorrhagic fever."

"I wish I knew what to say to make you feel better, Doc. But for what it's worth, you've come here for a reason. One day of work isn't going to give you the solution." Polly put a powder into a glass of water and swirled it around, then took a drink of the fizzing concoction.

Kit watched her; head cocked slightly. "What's the matter, not well?"

"After all that chili I ate tonight, got a bit of a stomach upset—and it's mild. Not like the stomach pains I've seen with the sickness people been getting. Stop worrying, Doc. I'm fine. Heartburn isn't terminal. I just need to get my mind off my troubles, and maybe you do, too." Polly gave her a big smile and leaned forward. Kit kept her eyes trained on Polly's.

Their faces were inches from each other. The air grew thick between them. Kit picked up her beer and took a long drink.

"You care for some company tonight, Doc?"

"No."

Polly sat back. Her smile faded into a wistful one. "Well, I tried."

"You did. It's not you, if that's any consolation. You're beautiful, even with your funny nose."

The blonde touched the tip of her own nose and laughed with a snort. "Oink, oink, Doc. If you're ever up for some bacon you know where to find me."

"Sleep well, Polly."

"Gonna be a long night, Doc."

Kit sighed, stood up, and put her hat back on as she went upstairs from the bar to the room that Polly set aside for her. A simple room with a bed, dresser, and a small washroom, but one with good plumbing. All along, Kit made a mental checklist of things the surveyors would need to look at and get samples—the storm drains, checking the sewer to make sure it wasn't spilling back into the water supply, the water supply itself, and surveying the people.

Oppressive heat surrounded the doctor like a second suit, and Kit stripped down to a light linen shirt. She opened the windows and looked out onto Main Street, below. There were few people outside now. Yina sat on the porch of the Sheriff's Office, a light on inside illuminating her and throwing shadows onto the wood slats. A man walked his horse to a trough and went inside the saloon where Kit couldn't see him. A few minutes later, she heard familiar grunts and groans and creaking wood from the bed frame moving.

She sighed, removing the last of her vestments and crawled into the warm, clean bed. She pulled the sheet up to cover her legs and hips, then left it, letting her top half remain exposed to the rapidly cooling night air.

Her locket clinked and she pulled it forward, moving the vial away from the oval pendant. Kit opened it and sighed, looking at the photo of a boy's round face and huge, sky-colored eyes and short-cropped black hair.

"I'm so sorry, Thomas. You're never far from my thoughts."

She closed her eyes, then opened them again.

It wasn't morning, but it might as well have been for the light streaming into the room from outside. It was as if the building was being consumed in fire, yet nothing was burning. The doctor sat up and looked around, rubbing her eyes. She leaned over, hands searching the nearby chair for her pocket watch. In the light, it wasn't difficult to find her waistcoat pocket to remove it.

"It's three in the morning, for Grimm's sake, what's going on out there?" Kit hopped out of bed and dressed quickly, hitching on her gun belt and checking her revolver in its holster. She stuck her head out the window and looked around.

It wasn't difficult for Kit to track the source of the glow, though she had to squint her eyes against it. To the north where the foothills swelled into the Pinebrook Mountains, a strong, yellow glow burst across the bumps, falling to bright white lights inside the caves.

Kit grabbed her shade-spectacles and put them on which eased the searing pain in her head. She closed her eyes a moment and squeezed them shut, then opened them again. The light faded a bit—either naturally or from her spectacles and eye adjustment—and Kit could make out the horizon once more. The caverns and foothills were awash in red, orange, and pink, with the backdrop of the night sky a dark purple. The mountain range looked like it was wearing a crown.

The scene reminded her of the old traditionalist's paintings of Alastor. His enlightened crown around his head was always depicted as a rainbow of colors, but particularly the reds.

She ducked her head back inside and shut the windows, then drew the shades. Faint lines of light managed to bend their rays around the shades, and spill onto her bed, to the floor, and pointed to the door.

Kit followed the rays.

The desert cooled so well at night that the chill settled onto her skin, and she pulled her hat down further to keep her head warm. Across the street, Diribe now sat on the porch of the Sheriff's Office, smoking and observing the newcomer to the town. His lion-like face remained neutral as she made her way over to him.

"It's been this way for some time," Diribe said. "Yina can sleep through it, but I can't, so we trade shifts around two."

"I thought I was dreaming, at first. When did it start, do you remember?" Kit leaned against the support beam of the porch, one foot on it, the other still on the last step. It joined her as she waited for an answer.

"We're not dreaming—I hope not, and nothing wrong with my memory," Diribe took a long drag from his cigarette, the heavy, sweet smoke filling the air as he exhaled. Kathryn took a breath, and he offered it to her.

She took it and smoked, then handed it back. Diribe gave her a soft smile and patted the bench next to him. Kit sat.

"It started exactly six months ago today," Diribe said between puffs of his cigarette. "At first, people were alarmed. Rightfully so. My father told stories about the sky at night during the war. It wasn't bad enough that we were killing our own brothers and sisters during the Great Strife, no. It had to be worse with the sky lighting up with sightings of who knew what."

Kit nodded. "So no illnesses or queer things happening?"

Diribe shrugged, a small smile creeping to his lips. "This is Platt's Gulch. Lots of queer things happen around here. But I think I know what you're getting at. Yes. At first when the glow started, nothing happened at all. Everyone was going about their daily business. But I notice things. I notice a lot of things."

"What did you notice?" Kit fished out a cigarette from her pouch and lit it.

They were silent for a moment, smoking. Diribe seemed to be gathering his thoughts as the orange glow became dim enough that Kit had to remove her shade-spectacles.

"Animals."

"Animals?"

"They started to disappear." Diribe shrugged. "Once in a while, a cow dog or maybe livestock will wander off, or get snatched up by coyote, and we'd find remains later, or the dog would come back, but not this time. This was three or four at a time, and they never came back. No remains, nothing."

"What did the townspeople say about it?" Kit put one leg up underneath herself and leaned back, watching the horizon as it grew dimmer. "They didn't mention the lights? The missing animals?"

"The lights made them mutter and mumble, but they kept about their business. They never saw a pattern. I did, but that was because all the farmers, cowpokes, and sodbusters would report to me, and not talk to each other about their stock. They don't live close enough to each other on the edges of the town, and most of them don't have the time to come into town for much more than their necessities. Or if they did see a pattern, they didn't panic about it. At least no one told me they did."

Kit nodded. "You would've noticed."

"I would." Diribe's statement sounded matter-of-fact to Kit's ears, rather than stemming from ego. "You'd notice, too."

"I'm keen on observation." Kit stretched her other leg out in front of her, spur whispering against the pine boards.

"Funny you wear spurs but don't have a horse. What happened to it?" Diribe put his cigarette in the ashcan. It hit the bottom with a sizzle as the water in the can put it out.

"Nothing. Didn't have a horse in the first place. These spurs were my grandmother's. I didn't want to leave them when I left. She used them out here, out west during the war. Till she realized they were cruel and unnecessary." Kit fingered the edge of the spur on the boot that was sticking out from beneath her.

"So you wear them to remember her."

"And to remember that there's no need to be cruel or take unnecessary action."

Diribe's face broke into a grin. "You're not the type who needs a reminder."

Kit stared straight ahead. Diribe stopped smiling and leaned forward.

"I see the past in your eyes, even when you're not looking at me, and wearing those things."

A thin whisper echoed in Kit's head. She sighed. "I know you do. But you want to trust me."

"I do. You'll earn it. I feel it." Diribe sat back and Kit handed him her cigarette. He took a pull from it down to his fingertips, then tossed it into the ashcan. Another sizzle.

"Did you see Slater tonight?" The doctor asked. Diribe nodded.

"Yes, ma'am. He told me about the possible stolen files. I questioned some of the aides that were on staff that night, but no one recalls him even doing an autopsy."

"A lifeless lead, then," Kit sighed.

"A bad pun, too," Diribe said, "but yes, a lifeless lead."

The glow died down entirely, leaving the two sitting in the yellowy light of the Sheriff's Office. Kit pulled her spectacles off and put them in her pocket. A drunk in one of the jail cells groaned, coughed, and fell silent again.

"It just does this, and no one seems to care?" The doctor motioned to the mountain.

"They don't know what to do about it, so they focus on their daily lives," he paused. "It's only a matter of time before we're all dead or insane, probably," Diribe turned his face to look at the mountain range. "I don't like where this is going, and there's nothing I can do about it, either."

Kit turned to look at the man and put one hand on his arm, giving it a squeeze. "Yes you can. You can keep people calm, and reasonable. You can help gather people to do research so we can get to the root of the problem. We start with boring, practical solutions—checking the water, making sure there's not a problem with the food we're eating. It's tedious work, but it needs to be done."

Diribe squeezed her hand back. "It'll be hard but I'll get Rice to knock off his nonsense. I can do that, at least."

"Rice? Oh, yes, that's the one who claims to be a man of Alastor, doesn't he?"

The sheriff nodded. "That old cult just won't die, no matter what we discover. There are people who think the deity actually existed."

"Well, let them, as long as they don't hurt anyone. Alastor was one of the more harmless ones. It's no matter. Eventually their kind will die out."

"I suppose they will. I'm watching him. Alastor may have been harmless but Rice is a twisted scrap of trash."

"Good thing we have you here, then—watching out for us." She took her hand back with one last squeeze, then stood up. "I think I need to get some more shut-eye. Come at this fresh as raw milk. See you in the morning, Sherriff."

"Rest well, Doc." Diribe gave her a brief wave as she went back to the saloon.

***

A knock on the door roused the doctor from her sleep. Sunlight peeked through her window shades, and Kit sat up, still clothed. She pulled on her socks and boots. Her left foot was missing. She looked down to confirm its presence—and there it sat, without feeling. Quick and steady hands massaged it and moved the foot around till the pins and needles started picking at her.

Another knock.

"Who is it?" Kathryn put one hand on her gun, ready to draw in case it wasn't a friendly visitor.

"It's Polly. I got you some breakfast."

Kit hobbled over to the door and opened it. A pristine figure greeted her in a starched, cornflower blue dress with a white apron that didn't have a speck of food on it. She grinned at the doctor. "Thought you might be hungry."

"You thought right," Kit patted her stomach, the chair beneath her making a quiet creak as she sat down. Polly set the tray on the small bedside table next to her.

"Well I'm gonna bring you breakfast each morning, then," Polly poured a cup of coffee while she spoke. "It was a rough night for you, I imagine. The glow outside shines right in here." She shooed at the shades. "I hope they helped."

"They did, Pol. Thank you." Kit took the cup of coffee and sipped it, then looked down at her plate.

"Thought a big breakfast of bacon, eggs, toast, and fried potatoes would be a good start to your day. That and the fresh apples and cider. Just about everything grows around here if you know how to plant it just right. The rest gets brought in by stagecoach. I think I said that last night." Polly kept talking as she made Kit's bed, and Kit watched her, catching up on the words after a moment.

The coffee acted like a serum against the slow-firing sensors of her morning brain. Kit drank it down and turned to her breakfast. "Thanks, Polly. But you don't have to do this every day. It's too much. I don't deserve this much hospitality."

Polly sat down on the made bed and shook her head. "That's a load of bullshit, Doc. You're here, you're helping us out, and you're not trying to sell us snake oil. Shut up and eat your breakfast."

Kit tucked in as she was told, studying Polly on the bed with sidelong glances.

"The lights—what do you make of them?" The doctor asked.

"Not much. Well, not too much. Nothing too unusual for around here—there's always something. If I got all in a twist about the Great Aurora or every dust devil that cropped up, I'd be fit for a straitjacket." Polly chuckled, then turned serious. "Are they something I should be worried about?"

Kit shook her head. "I doubt it. If things like this aren't unusual for Platt's Gulch, then it's probably nothing."

"Well, this wouldn't be the first time those lights came up, from what the M'aqual say. They've been here for decades, too. They say it happens from time to time." She shrugged. "You think there's a connection?"

The doctor didn't reply, just shook her head. Polly stayed silent.

When she was finished eating, Polly took her tray from her and headed out the door, turning once before departing. "I'll see you later."

"I mean it, Polly—you don't have to do this every day."

"No, I don't, but I'm going to. Besides, it gives me an excuse to spend time alone with you." She gave her a knowing look.

Before Kit could reply, Polly closed the door behind her with her foot.

Kit stood up and put on her duster, combed her hair, then headed out for the hospital, head full of ideas from last night.

The nurse's aides seemed relieved to see her when she walked through the door. The shift change left Kathryn with unfamiliar faces, but she recognized their uniforms and read their name tags.

Gemma, a petite, slender woman who had to look way up at Kit, wrung her hands as Hector told the doctor about the incoming patients.

"Three new ones," Hector said, motioning to their beds. "All with the same complaints. Stomach cramps like their innards have caught fire and general malaise. All of them running fevers."

"Are they related?" Kit started by looking over their charts. "Doesn't appear so."

"No, Doc. From different parts of town, too." Gemma was the one to reply and Kit looked over at her.

"What's wrong? Why are you so nervous?"

Gemma swallowed hard and shook her head. "I'm scared. I'm scared we're all gonna die."

Kathryn shook her head and leaned down. "Look at my eyes."

Gemma looked into Kit's eyes, and Kit listened to the whispers. It hurt to do it, but this seemed more important than a potential nosebleed. The sounds were a cacophony of worry, dread—the sinking feeling of the world around her slipping away as the void swallows the last bit of life. The woman's fears laid bare before her.

"Listen to me, Gemma. We all die eventually, and there's nothing to be done about that. You aren't alone—in death or in being afraid of it. But you need to be strong for these sick people. They need your words of comfort, not your fears. You have now—you have right now—to make a difference for them, whether they pull through or not. Does that make sense? Something to think about?"

The girl nodded and seemed to steel herself as she took in the doctor's words. The swirling, worried whispers ebbed.

"Now go home, go to bed, and get ready to be back here for your next shift. We need you." Kit patted her on the arm and turned her attention back to the patients, holding her nose closed with a handkerchief until she was sure there'd be no more blood oozing from her nostrils.

"Seemed like you knew exactly what to say to little Gem," Swifty's voice came from behind her. Kit turned and shrugged.

"Just lucky, I suppose. Good morning, by the way." Her face was stern, but her voice was soft. "We've got three more. That's thirty-six for the record."

"Yes we do," Swifty sighed and ran a hand through his hair. "Seems like we're never gonna stop this."

Kit shrugged. "I just got here, Slater. Give me a few minutes to solve it." She gave him a wry half-smile and took down some notes, then went to examine the three patients, handing Swifty the clipboards.

The questions Kit asked were long and tedious, the way most investigations into disease were. When did the symptoms start, what were they doing before they got ill, where did they get their water, what did they eat the days preceding the first symptoms, was there anything unusual, and more. Swifty took notes on everything.

The last patient was a little girl, nine years old. Kit's demeanor changed. She smiled at the child. "Hello there, what's your name, darling?"

"Willie Hayes," she said, then coughed.

"Well, Willie Hayes, I'm Kit. I'm a doctor. Tell me, what are you doing here?"

"I don't feel so good."

Kit asked the same questions of the girl that she did of the adults. Swifty watched and kept taking notes.

"Well, Miss Hayes, you get some rest. If you get better, we'll get you a nice treat. Do you like licorice?"

Willie's eyes got big. "I love licorice."

Kit took her pen light and leaned forward, looking into Willie's huge brown eyes. "Well you can have some when you get better, okay?" She moved to the little girl's ears and checked them with her otoscope.

"Yes, ma'am," Willie's expression went from excited to exhausted in a flash.

"I think I found part of the problem," Kit said.

"What? What is it?" Willie sounded hopeful.

"You've got something here," Kit's hands moved fast, and it seemed that she pulled a mini-book out of the little girl's ear, no larger than a matchbook. "Looks like one of those little comics. How did that get in there?"

Willie giggled and Kit smiled. "Here. You keep that and do all the puzzles in it if you feel bored. Don't forget to rest, though."

"Thank you, Doctor Kit," Willy said. She opened the tiny book and started reading the first puzzle.

Once they were done, Kit had her lips pursed together as if she'd tasted something sour, and she frowned hard enough to make Swifty take a step back when he looked up from his work.

"Doc, what's the matter?"

"Nothing. Walk with me, Slater."

Swifty hurried to take stride with the doctor and they left the sick ward, back to the doctor's office.

She had taken off her duster and hat before entering the ward, and they remained hanging on the coatrack. Kit reached into her duster's inner pocket and pulled out a tin, taking a piece of aspirin gum and chewing it. This time, *listening* decided to give her a headache. Those were only slightly better than the nosebleeds. At least the aspirin helped.

"You okay Doc?" Swifty glanced at the tin and back to her face. "You look like you gave birth to an angry porcupine."

"I'm fine. Just the trials of aging," Kit said, then took a seat at her desk. Swifty gave her a raised eyebrow and scrunched his face in confusion, then shook his head.

"Whatever you say, Doc. You still look young to me, and I *am* young," he pulled his chair up closer to the desk and rested his arms on it. "What's going on, then?"

"Tell me something, Slater. Did you notice anything unusual when the glow started?"

Slater's face did gymnastics feats in going from curious to grave. "Not at first, no. But I've been chewing on this for a bit now. The animals. Papa tends some cattle and Mama's crazy for cats because they keep the scorpions out of the house without using poisons. When the glow started, the cattle got nervous. Some ran off or disappeared."

"Right. Anything else?" Kit sat forward. "And don't tell me that this is a strange town. It wasn't this strange before the glow started; I could almost guarantee it."

"You're right, Doc. No, it's not out of the ordinary. The M'aqual have accounts of lights on the horizon, but not like this. Not like this at all. About six months ago, when the glow started, people started acting strange. Something people just write off because they have their own lives to live. But being here, I see things."

"What did you see?" Kit asked, not taking her eyes off the nurse.

"Billy Chen was a nice kid. Went crazy. Killed his whole family and blew his own brains out with a pistol." The nurse sighed and ran a hand through his hair. "He was thirteen."

"So just Billy Chen, or who and what else?" Kit pulled a map of the town down from the wall and put it on the desk. She took out a box full of pins, then handed the box to Swifty. "Here. Put a pin wherever there was unusual activity. Red head pins for anything older than four months, blue for four to three months, green for two months, and yellow for this month."

Swifty shook the box of pins to take out a handful and marked the map as he spoke. Kit watched him while she stood behind the desk, looking over his shoulder. "So here's the animals," Swifty said. Push. "Here's the Chen family." Push. "Here's where Daisy Mae Acorn threw herself down a sour well. Here's where Imini Dewdrop robbed the bank and ran off with Ana Stetson's baby." Push, push.

The man went on and Kit watched the pins, colors starting to form a pattern as Swifty described each incident that he could recall over the past six months. "And here's where Patient Zero lived. He—"

"Okay, stop. For all the sick patients, we need black pins." Kathryn pulled out another box full and handed it over to Swifty. "Show me all of them that you can recall over the past three weeks."

Swifty did as instructed, and when he finished, Kit looked down at the map and sat down. "Do you see the pattern?"

The nurse shook his head.

Kit shrugged and pointed it out. "Each black pin represents a sick person, yes?"

"Yes."

"Each sick person fell ill from a distance of exactly five miles apart in one direction or another."

Swifty heard what she said, but he looked up at her, mouth agape, as though the signal hadn't gone through. "They—" he looked back down at the map and put his fingers on one of the pinheads, pinching it hard enough to leave round indentations in his fingertips. "You're right."

"This isn't random," Kit said, sitting back in her chair. "This is something that's been planned out, surely."

"It could be coincidence," Swifty said, voice wavering.

"It would be one hell of a long shot, Slater. But let's go tend to our patients. Now we have something, though it's not much. Let's work with what we have."

***

When the sun began to make its descent below the horizon, Kit decided to call it a day, and set the nurse's aides with specific instructions.

"Push the fluids and if someone starts hemorrhage, do exactly as I instructed you during the beginning of your shifts. No aspirin to the patients who are already bleeding. Provide comfort and shots of morphine to those who request it. Make them as comfortable as possible. Palliative care only. I'll be back as soon as I can."

The nurse's aides gave head nods and 'yes, doctors' to indicate they understood, and Kit went back to her office. She checked her revolver, put on her duster, and hat. Taking a good long look around the room, she stalked off to the saloon for a quick dinner.

But Swifty was soon on her heels as she left the hospital doors and turned right to make her way up Main Street. "What are you doing tonight, Doc? What are you thinking?"

Kit kept walking. "Saloon. Supper."

"Oh no, you're not shutting me out, Doc." Swifty had to trot to keep up with her, but he managed. "There's no giveaway to your face, but you're seeing things that I'm not, and I deserve to know."

"You saw the pattern. You can put it together, Slater." Her boots hit the wooden walk that led to Polly's Saloon. A hand reached out and grabbed her arm. Kit pulled away and raised her fist.

"Don't ever, *ever* grab me like that, Slater." Kit's face turned into a snarl, but she lowered her hand when Swifty let go.

"I'm sorry, Doc. I'm sorry. I shouldn't have grabbed you." Swifty put his hands up in a defensive gesture, then lowered them. "I just want to know what's happening. I saw the pattern."

Kit didn't reply. She walked up the steps and into the saloon, sitting down in the far corner table, away from the crowd that'd gathered for the evening carousing.

Polly greeted her, but Kit's scowl kept the blonde at a distance. "I knew there'd be hard days, Doc. What can I get you to drink?"

"Just some soft cider with dinner, Polly, if you please." Kit took off her hat and put it on the seat next to her. She put her duster over the back.

Swifty made his way over to Kathryn, but people kept stopping him, asking him questions about the doctor and would more doctors be coming. Swifty told them they might, he didn't know, and that he didn't know much about the doctor except she was good at her job. Pat answers laid out, the nurse made his way to Kit's table.

"Can I join you, Doc?"

"Yes. Calm down. I'm not that pissed off, you know. I simply have an aversion to being grabbed."

"I was in the wrong. I just—"

Polly came over with a plate of steak, mashed potatoes, and mixed greens for each of them, and two huge mugs of cider. Kit and Swifty thanked her.

With just the two of them in the corner table, they seemed to have a bit of privacy. No need to raise voices. Still, Kit stayed silent, observing the plate in front of her, then tucking in. The table between them might as well have been an ocean. The ambient noise of the crowd accented by the clatter of silverware against ceramic, and the occasional dull thud of thick glass against wood as they drank the soft ciders.

"Slater, you look like a sick kitten," Kit said halfway through her meal. "Just ask me your questions and be done with it."

"I already asked you, Doc. What are you thinking? What are you fixin' to do?"

Kit swallowed a mouthful of cider before she spoke. "I'm going to the caverns. The glow, the disappearances, and Doc Harlan going mad, *and* the illnesses all surging with that glow in the sky? Not a coincidence, Slater, and you know it isn't." She punctuated her words with her utensils, then resumed eating.

Swifty let out a big sigh and put down his knife and fork. "I figure you're right, Doc. But it seems to me that Doc Harlan did exactly that and look what happened to him. You think the same won't happen to you?"

Kit shrugged. "What choice do I have? I can't just sit here and let people drop like raindrops around me. Besides, I'll be cautious. I'm telling you where I'm going. For all you know, Harlan went somewhere else entirely. I'm not going to disappear. But I'm going."

"What if we need you here? For an emergency?"

"The aides have been handling the emergencies, they'll continue to handle them. Besides, Diribe and Yana can handle those, too. And you can call on the doctor from M'aqual."

Swifty shook his head. "Nothing I can say to change your mind?"

"You've figured that out already." Kit took another drink.

"We should round up a posse, then," Swifty cut a piece of steak and chewed it, using his fork to animate his words. "Security in a group."

"No. I'm not going to let others endanger themselves just because I'm on a tear trying to find out what's killing Platt's Gulch." Kit dove into her potatoes and chased it with cider. "That's not fair to them."

"That's their choice to make, not yours, Doc." Swifty's cheeks bloomed circles of red.

"Getting angry with me isn't going to make me change my mind, Slater. You're not in charge of stopping this illness. I am," she punctuated her words with her fork. "That means I make the choices on what I do, and I'm going to investigate. I'm not rounding up a whole group. That would mean I'd have to be responsible for their safety and I'm going to be too busy to play nanny." Kit set her jaw and cut up her steak.

"And that's your final word." Swifty sighed and continued his meal.

"No. My final word is 'eat,' as in 'shut up and eat.'"

They finished the rest of the food in silence and Kit cleaned her plate, then polished off the last of her cider.

The cinnamon tickled her throat and she wondered if this might be her last meal.

"Doc, please don't do this." Swifty got up and walked a step behind her. He didn't reach out to grab her this time.

"I'll be back, Slater. I promise."

"I intend to see you keep that promise, Doc. I'm going with you."

Kit froze, then turned on her heel and looked down at Swifty. "Did you hear a word I said at the damn table?"

"Yes ma'am, but I don't need a nanny. I can take good care of myself and always have," Swifty shook his head at her. "You're *not* going alone. You can either ignore me the whole time, or we can work together. But you're sure as shit not gonna go out there by yourself."

She made a face at him. "What makes you think I can't take care of myself, Slater? I walked twenty-two hundred miles out here, alone. I survived. So now you're saying I can't?"

"I'm not saying that, Doc. Obviously you take care of yourself better than a lot of people, and I'm not trying to stop you, not exactly." Swifty set his jaw this time and looked at Kit with an edge she hadn't noticed before. His eyes were shining. Hard. “It’s just that—we can’t lose you like we did Doc Harlan.”

Kit sighed. “Fine. Let’s stop back at the hospital for a moment and grab our sample collectors. Make sure your gun’s clean and ready to shoot. Lots of wild animals out there, and the Unfriendlier. Found out the hard way those weren’t just stories.”

“Where’d you run into them? The Hills?”

Kit nodded.

“Wait,” Swifty took stride with the doctor as they headed down Main Street to the hospital. “You ran into the Unfriendlier and lived to tell about it?”

Kit shrugged and kept walking. Swifty’s eyebrows shot up.

“Damn, Doc. I guess you really could go out there alone.”

THE CAVERNS

The foothills rolled out in front of the two travelers as they kept in stride with one another, ground underneath going from flat and easy to bumpy and sloping upward. Crunching beneath boots gave their ears a rhythm that indicated the hardpan was giving way to rock and rubble.

Swifty carried a lantern. Kit wore a miner's strap with a light on it, curved around her hat. The beam lit a narrow path towards the strip of caves. Swifty swung his lantern so the golden light illuminated the periphery, checking for snakes that might be looking for places to get warm, or that had chosen a path of slumber.

"Should've brought our walking sticks," Swifty said, huffing out his words with each step.

"Should have. Didn't." The doctor pointed to the mouth of the largest cave. "We should probably start here and work our way inside."

Swifty stopped and stared at Kathryn. "We can't do that."

"Why not?" She kept walking toward the entrance. "Keep your voice down."

He lowered his voice to a whisper. "We can't do that because who knows what's in there. Could be people. Could be the Unfriendlier. Could be wild animals. The desert bear likes the caves."

"The desert bear is a myth, Slater. Made up to protect children."

"You thought the Unfriendlier were a myth," he said.

Kit shook her head. "Have you actually ever seen the desert bear?"

"Well, no, but I don't venture to the caves. Did once when I was a boy and I broke my ankle. Never came back here since." Swifty sighed. "It's a story to keep people away from the caverns, you're saying. A precautionary legend."

"It's a story to keep people away from the caverns, yes," Kit's repetition of what Swifty said was flat, and then she chuckled softly. "As if the caverns weren't dangerous enough." She took a deep breath and listened for the whispers of the Unfriendlier. Detecting none, she stepped forward.

"But people used to say the Unfriendlier were a myth, and those turned out to be real." He pointed out to the horizon. "Rare, but real."

"They're just people, Swift," Kit said. "Mutations just make their appearance a bit off. They keep to themselves, want to be left alone. Generations of inbreeding tainted their gene pool, and made them cautious to outsiders. Just leave them be. They take care of their own and are less dangerous than those cultists like Rice."

"Just no one's ever been able to talk about their encounters, Doc. They cut out tongues and slit throats for treading their territory. They're kind of like animals." Swifty shook his head. "But I don't see any to worry about."

"All humans are animals—don't do that to them. And no, I don't see any either. They like the areas where they can seek refuge from the sun, so be alert."

"Our real problem is there's that slipping sand in front of the cave openings. That's how I broke my ankle, way back then—fifteen years ago—on slipping sand." He showed Kit the sand under the golden glow of the lantern.

"See, it's like quicksand but it doesn't suck you down," Swifty took a small rock from near his shoe and tossed it underhanded at the slipping sand. It skipped and skittered over the sand, then rolled back down to Swifty's foot. "See? The sand moves and resists pressure, so you slip on it like it's vibrating. Like an earthquake."

"Fine, we'll just figure a way around it, then." Kit set her bag down on the ground and rummaged through it till she found her climbing rope. "We'll use this. Stand back."

Swifty gave Kit a wide berth as she swung the rope in an expanding circle. She tossed it up, over the cave's entrance, and started a slow pull.

The grappling hook skittered, making little ping noises as it went along. After a few minutes of pulling, it caught between two rocks. Kit pulled a little harder. Then harder still. It anchored.

"Okay. I'm going to swing over and throw the rope back to you. Can you do that and still hold the lantern?" Kit asked this while she was securing the rope around her wrists and hands, looping it so as to avoid burning when she swung.

"Yeah, I'll hold it in my mouth. It'll be fine." Swifty secured his belongings and nodded when he was ready.

"Okay. Don't wait. I don't know if those rocks will bear my weight, let alone yours." Kit shook her head. "Not meant as an insult."

"Not taken as one," Swifty chuckled. "I'm pretty slim but I'm heftier than you are, Doc. Go ahead."

Steadying herself on the other side of the slipping sand, Kit made a run and leapt across the natural barrier, holding onto the rope so she wouldn't slide down. She made it over the dip that would've cost her a broken ankle if she'd landed on it. Her boots made an echoing clack as they hit the bedrock of the cavern's opening.

Skidding, Kit used her spurs to stop herself from falling, and they made sparks against the ground. A whoosh of air came from her lips, and a grunt followed as she stopped.

Swifty opened his mouth to holler but closed it as he saw the doctor's expression—serious, as if she might kill him for whooping in excitement. Kit undid the rope from her hands and wrists, checked her belongings, then threw the rope to the nurse.

Without a word, she motioned for him to make his move when he was ready. Kit stood back and waited.

Beads of sweat broke out on Swifty's forehead as he checked the rope to make sure it had some give, but not too much. The rocks held the grappling hook fast.

Backing up a bit further than Kit had, Swifty gave himself a running start and leapt hard, lantern's handle clamped tight between his teeth as he went. He'd seen what Kit had done to keep herself from slipping on the cave's floor and tried to imitate her as best he could. Swifty's legs splayed out wider to support his frame, and he landed firm.

A grin spread across his face and Kit shook her head. "This is fun for you, isn't it?" she asked, her whisper making a hissing echo across the cavernous chamber.

"Gotta find the little pleasures, Doc." Swifty shrugged.

She took the rope from him and tied it inside to one of the jutting rocks. "So you say. Better to keep this in with us than let it dangle and give others a sign or a way to get in after us."

"I suppose you're right."

Kit looked around the entrance, on the walls littered with guano and moss. "Damp caves. This is the spring's source, I imagine." She listened with her ears this time. "I can hear the water dripping and the rush of the stream."

"Yeah, you've got good ears, Doc. I hear it too."

"I'm not that old, Slater, fuck's sake." Kit looked at the walls again. A dull red ink layered against the gray stone told tales of people, and large animals running after the people. Some of the ink told Kit words she didn't recognize, but there was a script of some sort. The language reminded her of the tattoos on Waya's body. "Is that M'aqual?"

Swifty turned to where Kit was pointing, holding up his lantern. "Yeah, it says, 'the way out.' So I suppose it's an exit sign."

Kit made a face that looked like a cross between surprise and amusement. "Exit. Indeed."

Swifty's face went from amusement to bemusement when he continued reading the lettering on the walls. "Look at this. This is ancient M'aqual. Got to be something like it. Maybe ancient, maybe another writing system. How about that?"

The doctor examined the writing. “I see the difference. Looks similar, but it isn’t. The lettering is more squared off, and the ink is faded. Some of it’s almost purple.”

“But this over here, Doc—this isn’t anything I recognize, and it looks even older. I’m obsessive about ancient M’aqual language, and this isn’t it.” Swifty didn’t touch the lettering but he held his lantern close and squinted. “Nope. This isn’t even vaguely related to M’aqual. Maybe the Unfriendlier’s language?”

Kit looked over Swifty’s shoulder and nodded. “I don’t know. It’s interesting, Slater, but I don’t think it really answers our dilemma. Come on, let’s go inside further.”

Swifty didn’t protest. He followed the doctor inside, getting out his collection bottles, in case Kathryn saw something worth sampling.

“Is it common to know M’aqual around here?” Kit asked.

Swifty bobbed his head in a simultaneous nod and shake, then shrugged. “Well, yes if you like to do trade with the elders. Loads of them don’t speak Albion’s language and won’t bother to trade with you if you don’t. They had bad run-ins with traditionalists for a while out here until the M'aqual government pushed the traditionalists out."

"Good," Kit said. "I have no patience for that traditionalist trash."

"I can tell. You know, the M'aqual leather goods are the best money can buy. Yaja's cousin—you know Yaja, right?"

"I do. Waya must've told you I was there at her home, then?"

"He did. Anyway, her cousin makes beautiful saddles that are so comfortable you can ride for days on them and fall asleep on your horse. Makes great chaps, too."

Kit let out a grunt of acknowledgement and Swifty went silent.

Stalactites and stalagmites stretched out to each other, making the cave look like it had sharp teeth in dozens of rows. Kit and Swifty stepped around them as they ventured deeper into the dark.

"Seems bigger on the inside," Swifty said.

Kit nodded. "Maybe it is. The cavern goes fairly deep. Feels cool in some places and warm in others. No telling how deep those spots go—so watch your step, Slater."

"I don't want another broken anything so long as I live, Doc, don't you worry."

"You might not just break something. A deep pit could swallow you whole and you'd never be found."

The sound of running water grew louder. Not a drip anymore, nor a trickle. It was the flow from a river, rushing near them and echoing through the cave.

They stopped underneath an arch and looked into what seemed like an impossible sight—in the next 'room' the water was flowing down, making an indoor river, fed by a waterfall that appeared to be emerging directly from the chalky stone. The water fell hard, like the mill she used to love to watch as a little girl on her father's shoulders. During their walks, she'd make him stop to watch the miller's wheel, water dancing off the paddles, silvery and golden in the light of day.

Here, the only illumination was the light they carried. The water took on a sinister quality, looking almost like oil against the lamps.

"This is the water that feeds Twist River," Swifty said, moving his lantern over the water. "No guano in here."

"The noise bothers them," Kit said. "They're too bright to use the stream as a toilet." She indicated with a gesture to the top of the waterfall. "See that? The chalk filters the water. It's what keeps it clean, but we'd better check to see if it's tainted away from the fall."

She snapped on a pair of gloves and took one of the collection bottles from Swifty. Bending with care, Kit took a sample of the river water and capped it tight, then handed it back to him. "Make sure it gets swathed so the glass won't break if you drop it, alright?"

But when she turned, Swifty wasn't with her—he was gone.

Kit's face fell and she felt a shiver run down her spine. With one hand on her revolver, she put the bottle on the ground and looked around. She didn't speak. Instead, she observed.

Movement, then nothing. The shadow went beyond the bend of cave where she couldn't see. Light didn't bend around corners.

Kit inched forward, along the side of the cave wall. She pulled her gun from its holster. Her hand tightened around the grip.

The double-action revolver didn't need her cocking back the hammer, although it was nice to be able to do that when she had to threaten someone. This time, she just kept her trigger finger close to the guard and investigated.

She found Swifty, alone, bent over something that glinted against the lantern.

"What in Perdition are you doing, Slater?"

Swifty looked up at her. "Look at this, Doc. I found something strange." He dusted off the find and moved to the right so she could stand next to him and have a look.

A piece of metal. Kit scoffed. "You scared the white lights out of me for a piece of—what is it?"

"I don't know, Doc, but it's not like anything I've seen, myself." Swifty picked it up and turned it over in his hand. "It's smooth. Really smooth. Like sword metal, only it's got some give to it." He bent it, and the metal snapped right back into its original bend.

"Take it with you, but be careful, Slater." Kit handed him her bandana. "Here. Don't keep handling it. We don't know what it is and for all we know that could be part of our problem."

Swifty opened his mouth to protest but took the bandana from her and wrapped up the metal in a sack before putting it away.

"Arguing with you is worse than arguing with a mule, isn't it?" Swifty closed up his bag and washed off his hands in the stream. "Damn, I sure hope I don't get sick."

Kit gave him a grave look. "If you do, I will too. At least you won't go alone."

"That's a comfort," Swifty said.

"And yes, it is, by the way." Kit grinned a little.

Swifty looked confused. "'It is' what?"

"Arguing with me is like arguing with a mule. Actually, it's worse," Kit said. "I can speak and I kick a lot harder."

She walked back to where she dropped the second water sample, bent down, and picked it up. "Take this one, too."

The ground gave a groan, and the two looked around as the noise echoed in the chamber of the cave. Their eyes settled on each other.

"Earthquake?" Swifty asked. "Haven't had one of those in years."

"I don't want to stick around and find out."

The ground shook again and Kit and Swifty swayed with it, running as the ground tried to slide them back and forth.

Cracks opened and pieces of rock and rubble fell, leaving plumes of dust in their wake. Kit and Swifty took in lungs full and coughed as they made a break for the entrance.

"Hurry!" Kit ran in long strides, grabbing the rope as her legs pumped in defiance of the ground.

She grabbed Swifty around his waist and he put his free hand on the rope. They ran in stride with one another, jumping as they got to the edge.

Swifty's size carried him further than Kit with his momentum, and Kit slid on the slipping sand, still holding the rope. Swifty let go and landed on his knees. The doctor landed on her backside and sprung up on her feet at the 'v' where the ground met the foothills. She rolled as the ground shook.

Breathless, Kit reached out to Swifty and they helped each other up as the earthquake stopped, and all was silent.

"Are you hurt?" she asked, dusting herself off and looking over Swifty's body.

"No. I'm fine. You?"

"I seem to be unscathed. Bottom's sore but it'll pass."

Swifty coughed to cover a chuckle but said nothing when he saw her give him a sidelong glare.

***

In the warmth of the hospital, the sounds of patients, awake and miserable, filled the room out to the hallway. Kit and Swifty were greeted by a nurse's aide. Her nametag read: Jessica.

Jessica was a petite girl with dark brown hair and dark blue eyes. When she smiled, the apples of her cheeks took on a charming blush. "Doctor, Swift—are you both well?"

"We're fine, Jess," Swifty said, reaching out to pat her on the arm. "Just a bit shaken up, literally."

"Oh, well, the patients are awake and disturbed. Some are starting to bleed. But we're trying to make them comfortable and settle down. Alex is preparing shots of morphine for them."

"Good," Kit nodded her approval. "We're here for the lab. If you need us, though, Jessica, you'll know where to find us. Call on me if it gets to be too much."

"Yes, Doctor." Jessica opened the doors to the ward and the swell of moans and complaints grew.

"I guess the earthquake really disturbed them," Kit said.

Jessica stopped with the doors halfway open. "What earthquake, Doctor Judge?"

Kit and Swifty looked at each other, then back at the nurse's aide.

"The one we just had a few minutes ago," Swifty said. He cocked his head. "Didn't you feel it here?"

Jessica shook her head. "No, sir. Guess we were lucky."

"You mean to tell me they just woke up and started acting out?" Kit raised an eyebrow at Jessica.

"Yes, Doctor. It was as if something woke them but we didn't feel a quake here." The young woman raised her hands in an 'I don't know' gesture.

Swifty looked up at Kit, who chewed on her bottom lip and gave him a dark look. "Let's off to the lab, Nurse Slater."

The pair left Jessica behind to tend the infirm and shut the pathology doors behind them. Kit leaned against where the doors met, closed her eyes, and sighed. "So it wasn't an earthquake. That would've been felt all the way down here if it had. Wouldn't you agree?"

Swifty shrugged. "I'm inclined to agree, Doc. That felt like a big enough quake to reach the Gulch, and if they didn't feel it here, well, that'd be strange. Unless it was far enough away for us to be on the edge of it."

"I suppose you're right. Still, it was strong enough—" Kit shook her head. "I suppose it's not important. Still, a bit strange. You say there haven't been quakes here in some time?"

They changed into sterile lab coats, gloves, goggles, and skullcaps as they spoke.

"Not for a decade, at least, Doc." Swifty tucked loose strands of his dusty brown hair under the cap, then changed gloves. "I always forget about my straggly hair. Pay for it by going through more gloves than I should." He sighed. "Someday I'll remember."

"At least you remembered before touching the equipment, Swift." Kit removed the objects for testing—water and soil samples—and Swifty removed the sheet of unusual metal. "See if you can get some scrapings off the metal and use the power scope. Hope the town doesn't mind us using so much electricity." The doctor smiled. "They're probably motivated for me to cure this. Which reminds me—do you have a mayor?"

"No. He died ten years ago and we decided we were better off without them. The Sheriff runs the show around here and we elect him to do it. Diribe and Yina are both elected, actually, and they pretty much appoint people to do work for us. Like the electricity and sewer. The boring things no one else wants to do. Just about everybody pitches in though." Swifty took several swabs from a jar and rubbed them against the metal sheet. "I was fifteen when the mayor died. He was a traditionalist. Got himself killed in a duel with some other traditionalist. Some argument over something or other with Nico Rice."

"The cultist?" Kit looked up from her water samples. "He's got away with it?"

"Well, yeah," Swifty cocked his head. "It was just a duel. It's not considered murder out here when it's a duel. I don't know what it's like back East, though."

"I don't suppose it's murder if it's a formal duel but we haven't had one in over fifty years, I don't think. If they did, they didn't come to me to help them." Kit went back to her water samples. Soon the only sound was the clattering of glass and metal as they worked to prepare slides and tubes.

Swifty stole glances at Kit while they worked. The doctor seemed consumed with her tasks in front of her, making sure everything was done with precision.

"Why'd you come out here, Doc?" Swifty put his samples in the testing tray and slid the tray into the power scope. The machine made a light whirring noise as it accepted the samples.

"Because you needed physicians."

While the power scope analyzed the material, Swifty sat back and watched Kit prepare her samples for viewing next. "But how did you know we needed you? It's not like we put out an advertisement all the way out East."

"It wasn't Platt's Gulch I was looking for—not at first. I just heard through the wire that people out West needed doctors, so I decided to venture out. Then later I heard about this place. So I came here. Why? You're not happy to see me?" Kit looked serious for a moment, then grinned. "I'm not always so grave."

Swifty waved a hand in her direction. “That’s fine, Doc. Not saying we’re not glad for you around here. Just wondering about you. You seem like you keep a lot to yourself.”

“I do. My life is my business, Slater. Just like yours is to you.”

They fell silent and got back to their work.

***

Swifty slammed his fist down on the table. “Damn it all to Perdition. I thought for certain we’d find something. Clean water, clean metal. Nothing.”

“Not ‘nothing,’ Slater,” Kit said, removing her skullcap and finger-combing her hair out of its bun. “Now we know what’s not infecting the people. It’s something. We can move onto searching for another cause and eliminating it.”

She put her hand up to her forehead and massaged it, then sighed. “It’s discouraging in its way, but we can’t give up.”

“You don’t sound convinced, Doc.”

“Just tired,” the doctor pulled out her pocket watch and checked the time. “It’s almost three in the morning. I’m going back to my board and getting some rest. You do the same. See you back here around eight."

Kit and Swifty parted ways outside the hospital. She headed for the Saloon—Swifty to his home on the outskirts of town. He mounted his horse and bid the doctor goodnight.

As Kit walked, she took in the sight of the town in the weak lamp glow of Main Street's lights, and sighed. The streets were quiet, most gone home or to sleep. A familiar black horse eyed her as a man she knew as Overton led him to Still's stables.

The feeling that the horse was making eye contact weighed on Kit, and she nodded her head at the mare, and then Overton. It seemed as if the horse nodded back along with the man. *I must be overtired,* she thought.

She passed Yina at the Sheriff's office and waved. Yina waved back and lit a cigarette.

The glow of that cherry hit the doctor as if she'd fallen into frozen water, stopping her pace for a moment as she looked into the distance, to the horizon full of fat stars and black sky.

There's no glow tonight.

She headed up the steps to Polly's Saloon and came in through the boarder's entrance, then took the stairs two at a time with ginger steps. Her door creaked as she opened it, and she stepped inside.

With the windows open, a cool breeze swept through the room and Kit undressed, putting on a nightshirt and climbing into her bed. Still no glow.

The locket clanked against her chest, and she put one hand on it, then opened it. She admired her boy's dark hair, and the eyes that were her blue. She could even recall the spray of freckles on his nose, and the way his nose crinkled when he laughed.

Laughter into coughing and coughing into blackness. Kit floated along on her bed down a clean river and into a furnace.

She woke with sunlight streaming in through the east window and sat up, covered in a thick sheen of sweat. Throwing the sheets to the side, she fanned herself off as she got dressed, then opened the door and the window for a cross-breeze. The oppressive heat began to vanish, replaced by a cooler breeze from the window.

The trolley that Polly used clanged along the floor as she rolled it toward Kit's room. "Well I thought you were fixin' to sleep all morning," she said to the doctor. "You came in so late last night."

"Why? What time is it?" Kit felt around for her pocket watch and extracted it.

"It's only seven-thirty," Polly said, dishing out a spoonful of honey and spreading in over Kit's pancakes.

She looked at her watch, confirmed the time, and put it away. "Looks good, but I need to hurry, Pol. I should be at the hospital by eight."

"That's okay, Doc. I know you're working hard. But don't overwork yourself." Polly patted her shoulder. Kit stiffened, but not by much.

"Thanks, Polly. I won't." Kit tucked into her breakfast, eating as much as she could in just a few minutes.

"I worry about you, Doc. You can't get by on just a few hours of sleep." Polly said, voice almost chastising but tipped with concern.

Kit snickered. "I'm well accustomed to no sleep for a few days," she said. "Medical school puts one through their paces."

"That's fair enough, but even the finest doctor has to stop and rest now and then."

"I'll rest soon enough. But if I don't keep going now, Polly, more people will rest for good." She stood and grabbed her medical bag. "If you'll excuse me."

Polly nodded. "Of course, Doc. Have a good day." She took Kit's trolley and backed out of the room. Once Kit was sure she wasn't going to try to come back for more conversation—or a lecture, the doctor left.

***

Swifty turned up at the hospital later than Kit did, but she said nothing. Instead, she finished her rounds and headed back to her office. When the nurse was ready, he joined her there.

"Did you notice something funny about last night?" Kit asked as Swifty sat down with an armload of charts.

"Not really, no," Swifty said. He scrunched his lips and thought about it. "Got home with my horse and Papa was waiting up for me. He pretends he doesn't worry and that he's fixing things, but I can tell he's full of it."

"So, you didn't see the sky, then," Kit took some of the charts and reviewed them as she spoke. She looked over the top of one at him. "Anything different?"

Swifty opened his mouth to say no, he hadn't, but closed it again and snapped his fingers. "The glow."

"The glow."

"It wasn't—well—it wasn't 'on' last night." Swifty ran a hand through his hair and sighed. "Is that right, Doc?"

"Yes. There was no glow. Also, this morning, what did you notice?" Kit looked at him, eyebrows raised and eyes wide, as if to prompt him.

"Nothing, Doc. Just business as usual."

"Not nothing, Slater. Something. That nothing is something." The doctor jotted some notes down on one chart and passed it back to him, taking the next one. "There weren't any new patients last night."

Swifty looked like she'd just kicked him somewhere tender. He swallowed. "You think they're related?"

Kit shrugged. "They might be, or not. It could be entire coincidence. I've not been here but a couple of days. If we observe for a week, a pattern might emerge. Meanwhile, people will die while we wait to find out. It's a terrible thing—to have to play a game of wait-for-it and find out if those things are related." She rubbed the back of her neck and sighed.

"I know, Doc. It's making the people restless and when they get restless, they get ugly."

"What people don't know is that rushing ahead gets more people killed than it does good," Kit said as she leaned forward. The vial around her neck made a soft clack and she set her jaw. "So it's best if you don't rush. We'll concentrate on tending the sick as we observe their symptoms and try to find what's causing this. Perhaps the answer is still under the power scope, perhaps not. You ken my meaning?"

Swifty nodded. "I'm with you, Doc. It's best if we don't answer a lot of questions from people, either. They do tend to gossip and you know that'll just make things worse."

"Agreed." Kit signed off on the rest of the charts and handed them back to Swifty. "Observe and report. For now, it's all we can do."

"And what about Rice?" Slater gestured to where the cultist kept his court and the meeting hall. "What about them?"

"They're just people, Swift. We treat them the same as anyone else. If they're sick, we treat them here. If they're healthy, we go about our business. Why? Are they a cause for concern?"

A long pause. Slater looked out the office window as if he could see Rice inside the walls of the meeting hall. "No. I suppose not."

"Then business as ordered," Kit said, rising to her feet. "We do our best and hope it's enough."

***

Little black dots from the pins that indicated the sick began to grow again, and the pattern remained within a five-mile radius of one another. Kit stared at the Slater for a moment, her gaze hard. "The glow nights seem to be random on their own, or we're not waiting long enough to establish a pattern. It seems to be every couple of days. The illness, however ..."

Kit marked areas of significance on her map and matched them to her calendar. On the nights the sky was awash with glow, the next morning, two or three unrelated people would come in with symptoms. Still within a five-mile radius of one another. The nights without the glow proved to have no one.

"It's gone on so long, Doc, that I don't think anyone's really noticed. We just got used to it when it seemed like nothing came of it." Swifty heaved a huge sigh and buried his face in his hands.

"Slater, that's human nature. You can't blame yourself for not seeing it. You're one person, and you were in it. I was a newcomer, looking at it with an outside observer's distance." Kit leaned back in her chair. "These are people you care about, I assume."

"Many of them—the ones I know well, anyway." Swifty looked up at the doctor. "You either pretend you don't care about them, or you actually don't care about them. I can't tell which."

"No. Neither applies, Slater. I have a distance. This isn't my home. I didn't put down roots here or raise a family or marry someone from here. I came into town and found a puzzle to unlock. That's all." Kit shook one hand at the nurse, seeing an almost appalled expression on his face.

"Now that doesn't mean I don't care. It just doesn't do any good to get emotional about it. I can't ask you to distance yourself, Slater, but I can ask you to tap into your professional reserves in order to help these people recover. Weeping at their bedsides won't help a bit. Applying action to their problems— alleviating their suffering by solving this puzzle will."

Swifty let go of the breath he'd been holding and put his hand over his eyes, then ran his hand through his hair. "You're right, Doc. It's not easy, but you're right."

She looked over one of the charts. "Speaking of recovery, our mortality rate is still at a-hundred percent, isn't it?"

Swifty clenched his jaw and nodded. "Yes'm, it is."

"This is unprecedented. Even the most virulent plagues leave behind survivors, or people who are simply immune because of their body's defenses or some other hostile environment to the invader." Kit shook her head. "This could be the start of something we can't control, but at least for now, we know it's not contagious."

"That's true. But do you think it could become contagious?" Swifty got a little pale and rocked forward, then sat back. To the doctor it looked like he was having an internal battle—a thin whisper came into her head as she observed him.

"No, Slater. It doesn't really work that way, or rather I've never seen a spontaneous mutation of that nature. Even though I haven't seen this before doesn't mean it's going to behave abnormally." She shrugged. "Although I can't guarantee that. There are no guarantees in medicine, as my father liked to say. Generally, though, no."

Kit fell silent and the two sat for a moment.

"That wasn't reassuring, was it?" Kit asked.

"Not really. Well, in a way, maybe it is." Swifty said.

"How so?"

"You're being honest. When you don't know something, you say so. You make me remember that we're fighting an unknown, but we're not alone." Swift gave her a small smile.

"No, we're not alone." Kit nodded.

"What do we do now?" Swifty spread his hands in a questioning gesture.

"I think we should wait for a glow night, and go visit the caverns," Kit said.

"Are you out of your mind, Doc? Isn't that a little like running towards a bear when you're unarmed, or jumping into a pit of rattlers?"

"Yes and yes, but do you have any better ideas?"

"I don't." Swifty sighed.

"You don't have to go with me, Slater. I've done over two-thousand miles on foot, alone, and I can do more. I won't take it personally if you don't feel safe going. In fact, I think you're sane not to go." Kathryn put another black-headed pin in the map.

"I'm going. In for a morsel, in for the meal." Swifty ran a hand through his hair and stood up. "Besides, I can't live with myself if I don't go with you. Not because you can't take care of yourself, but because I'd think of myself as a coward."

"Fine. Watch the sky tonight, Slater. When the glow starts, we start. You'll meet me at the saloon. Bring as much as you can."

Swifty gave her a thumbs-up. "You got it, Doc."

"Oh, and Slater?"

"Yes'm?"

"What've you got against bears?" The doctor smiled at him. Swifty blushed.

THE GLOW

Kathryn stood outside, smoking a cigarette and leaning against one of the support posts at Polly's Saloon. The air chilled her face with each gentle breeze, and the sun dipped down below the horizon just a bit earlier than it had before. This part of the country didn't have the change of seasons, but the days got a little cooler, just the same. It made for comfortable evenings watching sunsets as fresh tobacco smoke perfumed the air.

A change of seasons, from hot to cold, she supposed.

As soon as Kit had finished her dinner at Polly's, she gathered her testing equipment and watched for sunset. Once the darkness settled over the town, she waited—a narrow-shouldered figure staring out her window.

After about an hour or two of gazing at the horizon, the glow started. It wasn't as bright as it had been when Kit awoke those many nights ago, but it was present, and getting stronger by ticks of the clock as time wore down.

She slung her bag over her shoulder, checked her revolver, and headed out the door to wait for Swifty.

Looking around Main Street, Kit drew deep from her cigarette and did something she was good at: observing without being obvious.

People were not about the streets at night, and not even the Sheriff or Deputy were out on the porch this evening. Perhaps it was too cold, or perhaps they were investigating something. Kathryn made no move to find out.

Instead, she thought about the past week or so, and what the surveyors brought back to her as information. It was like putting the edges of a jigsaw puzzle together. Once she had the frame, then perhaps she might be able to put the rest of it into place.

On the nights where people got sick, the families reported, nothing seemed out of place. Layer after layer, the doctor reviewed the cases over and over in her mind. Person after person told her that they hadn't done or seen anything unusual. It seemed to her that nothing in the pile stood out.

Except for one report.

Just one, and Kit thought it might be the answer to one of the missing pieces.

June Regret was the missing piece.

June's sister, May, had never married either, and the sisters lived together and kept an apiary. Regret's Honeybees seemed like an unfortunate name to Kit's ears, but it was still good honey.

After a long day, June told May she was going for a walk. May was tired.

"I'm going to retire early. Come back without making noise if you can help it—you know how I am."

"A gentle wind will wake you up, but I'll give it my best," June said. "Perhaps sleep under the pillow." She said. "The scantest sounds wake you."

"Don't chide me," May said, but she smiled at her. "I'll stuff cotton in my ears if I can find any. Go on then, and don't be too long."

June, considerate of her sister, agreed and went on her walk. May readied herself for bed and laid down, staring first at June's empty bed, then watching the clock on the end table tick away the hours. It was around eight o'clock when her lids grew heavy, and the monotonous noise carried her to sleep.

A sharp click of the front door caused May's eyes to snap open, still facing the clock. Its face read four in the morning.

She sat up and looked at her sister meandering into the room.

"That was some walk, June," May said, voice scolding. "You'd best be careful walking about like that so late at night."

"I don't feel so like myself," June sighed, standing in the middle of the room. May thought she swayed a little on her feet. "I need to lie down."

"Come here," she said. "I've got you." May got up and brought her sister to her own bed and helped her into it. June felt hot, and when May turned up the lights in the room, she could see her sister was flushed.

"I think you've gained a fever, JJ."

"Fever. Yes. It's a fever." There was something so hollow about June's reply that May shivered.

"You don't sound like yourself. What's wrong?"

"I'm—I just feel strange." She shrugged out of her vest and garments, leaving them on the floor in front of her. May picked them up and placed them in the laundry basket.

"I can tell. You're not concerned about being messy." She smiled at her sister, but her face fell when her sister coughed, a trickle of blood falling from the corner of her mouth.

"Did you bite your lip, Junie?" May's eyes narrowed as she dabbed at her sister's face with the cuff of her robe.

"I don't know. I just need to lie down. Please."

"Of course. Come on, dear. Let's clean up a little bit and tuck you in. You probably just need to sleep." May poured a glass of water from the pitcher and dabbed a napkin in it, then wiped the runner of blood from her sister's face. "I can't see where you cut it or bit it, but you'll be fine. You probably exerted yourself being out there eight hours."

Three days later, May took June to the hospital, and June died from a massive gastrointestinal hemorrhage the day after.

Kit took a deep drag from her cigarette and scanned the south for where she expected to see Swifty, probably on his horse. The Regret Sisters still stuck with her. She was hearing their whispers—May's fervent prayers that if Alastor really did exist, would he please help June and cure her, and June's fearful and pained complaints of wanting the pain to stop, not wanting to die, and then, eventually, begging for death to come.

When she heard June die, she was almost as relieved as June was. Relieved for the quieting of the whispers.

She tried to shake the thoughts away with another shiver and whittled her cigarette down to her fingers. Satisfied, she crushed the embers on her bootheel and tossed it into the ashcan.

The clop of horse hooves got her to look up and to the south. Swifty rode in on a brilliant palomino, stopping just in front of the doctor.

"Magnificent beast," Kit said, holding up one hand in greeting to the nurse. "She's just beautiful."

The horse nosed at Kit's upheld hand, and the doctor responded by stroking the horse's muzzle. "Hello, Sally."

"What's that, Doc?" Swifty said as he climbed down from the horse. "Did you say something?"

"No, I didn't. What's her name?"

"This is Sally," Swifty smiled and patted the horse's neck. "She's a good horse. Likes to work and run."

"She's a brilliant girl," Kit said. The horse nickered.

“I think she likes you, Doc. She doesn’t usually like people. Well, I mean, people she doesn’t know.” Swifty shrugged. “I guess she knows you through me, maybe. She can smell you on me. I mean—uh—”

“You mean from the hospital. I understood.” Kit chuckled. Even in the soft glow of the foothills and streetlamps, she could see that Swifty was blushing. “Are you planning to ride her to the caverns?”

“No, ma’am,” Swifty shook his head. “I figured I’d ride her here and then keep her hitched to Polly’s till we got back.”

Kit shook her head this time and waved towards the stablehouse. “No. Take her over to Still’s and keep her there for the night. If we don’t make it back, someone will take care of her till your parents come get her.” She reached into her bag and fished out some paper money. “Here. Pay for it with this. Tell him you’re spending the night at the saloon with me and that you don’t want to be disturbed, maybe for a couple days.”

Swifty cocked his head and gave a lopsided grin that looked more confused than amused. “Why, Doc?”

"Because I'd rather have them up to gossip about dalliances between a doctor and nurse than trying to follow us into the foothills where they might get killed faster. Think about it, Slater. They come looking for us, then they're just as doomed as we might be." Kit kept her voice low and leaned in close. "Just humor me."

"Alright, Doc." Swifty swallowed hard, then took Sally's reins and carted her off to Still's Stables. Kit didn't need his whispers to understand what he was thinking.

When he returned, he gave Kit a huge grin. "Well I got some congratulations all around for getting to say I'm spending a couple nights with you, Doc."

Kit gave a wry smile. "I'm not sure whether to be flattered or not."

"I sure am."

The doctor walked north and Slater followed. "Let's try a different entrance this time, one of the spots we didn't search when we were there last. Does that slipping sand go all the way around the foothills?" She pointed in the direction of the cave system.

Swifty trotted to catch up with her and caught the last of what she said. "Yeah, pretty much, Doc. But I brought rope and grappling hooks for us so we could navigate the area."

"Good. We'll need them."

They took their walk in silence and Kit tried to shut out Swifty's whispers. It helped when she focused on the mountains and the glow that was getting stronger with every step the pair took. In fact, it was a lot easier to shut out his whispers than it was with other people.

As they drew closer, the glow grew in intensity. Kit put her hand out and stopped Swifty from going further.

"Let's not go barreling in like a couple of young shavers," she said, then gestured just off to the west. "Over there. It looks like the glow is the strongest. We'll start over there."

Swifty put one hand over his stomach. "Guts got a pit in them today."

"Literal or metaphorical?" Kit gave him a look pinched with concern, but he waved her off.

"Metaphorical. I just have a bad feeling about this."

Kit shrugged. "As do I, but there's little else we can do about it, Slater. It's either forge ahead or give up."

Swifty nodded, then set his jaw. "I won't give up."

"Good. Let's go."

They moved on quick feet to the west of the foothills and stole their way to the small entrance.

"The challenge will be greater because the opening is narrower," Kit used her hands to indicate the size difference between the large, more central cave and the small one. "We're more likely to get banged up hopping across the slipping sand."

Swifty bit his lower lip. "I'll go first. There's a bit of a ledge to this one—you can see where it rises off the ground if you tip your light over here."

Kit followed where Swifty indicated. "I see it. Fairly steep, actually."

"Yup." The nurse tossed his grappling hook and pulled gently on the rope just as Kit had done days ago. His movements were blunt, determined, but effective. He didn't say another word and took a running start to hop from one side of the sloping landscape up onto the ledge. He tripped and caught himself in time to roll on the ledge and bang into the side of the entrance.

The doctor followed suit but didn't have as much difficulty navigating the ledge. This time, she didn't slip as she had before, and landed soft, stopping herself just before she hit the other side of the narrow entrance.

They took the ropes up and brought them inside as best they could. Kit had to squint for a moment to adjust to the light change. After a minute, she looked over at Slater and pointed to her lamp, then turned it off. She pointed to his lamp, making the same gesture for him to turn his off, too.

"If you say so, Doc," Swifty said, following suit. Kit put her finger over her mouth to shush Swifty, and motioned to him to follow her, then patted her hip. *Stay by my side.*

Swifty gave her the thumbs up to indicate he understood and joined her just behind.

What the caves didn't show the other night in the dark, they showed in the brilliance of the glow. It was bright as day inside the cavern network, and even the potential pitfalls were illuminated. Kit skipped over them, making soft landings, then edged close to the walls.

Looking ahead, the pair saw that this part of the caves had been changed—unlike the natural setting they'd seen in the center, the west appeared to have been renovated.

But by whom?

Inching forward bit by bit, the doctor led the way into what seemed to be an unoccupied area on the inside of the cave. The 'rooms' made a wraparound, almost a perfect U-shape that appeared too planned to ever have been natural.

Kit stepped forward into the small room and looked around. She didn't understand what she was seeing. View panels? Yes, some kind of view panels such as the one on her power scope at the hospital, but far more sophisticated. They didn't just give out pictures, but color pictures, graphs, and readouts that had equations on them.

On the tables in the room, there were Bunsen burners, test tubes, and other accoutrements Kit associated with pathology. She reached out and gripped Swifty's arm.

Don't touch anything, she mouthed at him. *Get out.*

They left the room on tiptoe, trying to escape without touching or interacting with any of the sophisticated equipment they saw.

"I don't understand what that was," Swifty whispered to Kit once they were out of the room and into the narrow passage that wound its way back to the center entrance. "It—it looked like a laboratory, but not one I'd ever seen before."

"I haven't seen anything like it, either," Kit said. She frowned and stayed to the side of the passageway, looking back and forth to make sure they didn't have unwanted company. Seeing no one about, she crept forward with Swifty behind her. He was so close, she could feel his body heat in waves. "I have so many questions I don't know where to start."

"What was all that equipment? Power scopes, I guess. But there were other instruments, too. Things that looked like surgical implements, maybe. And where were the people?" Swifty waited for Kit to answer him, but she said nothing. She had one hand on the butt of her gun, and the other was waving at him to be quiet.

He quieted.

The caverns led to what looked like a steep drop, and it reminded Kit of the surgical theater where she did her internship. The seats for observation of the operation were on risers, and a student could sit as much as twenty feet above the operating table to watch the procedures. She preferred to be as close as possible, but for the faint-hearted, the risers were the best option, as providing distance in space provided distance in emotion.

Kit got down on all fours and crawled to the edge with deliberate movements. The glow was the strongest coming from the drop.

Swifty came up alongside her and mimicked her movements. She looked to her right and gave him a grave nod.

Moving with purpose and stealth, they came to the edge and looked over, squinting in anticipation of the brightness.

They didn't need to squint. The glow wasn't brighter in the middle—it was emanating from the arc of the circular amphitheater—the naturally occurring one. Inside the circle, it was brilliant, but less so.

Two people were lying on operating tables inside some kind of artificial room, masks over their faces with tubes running up their noses and out their other orifices, even their ears.

The top of the artificial room was transparent, like glass—but not reflective. Kit and Swifty could see through it with ease.

A low hum came from the center of the construct, and over that, a series of chirps, whirs, and beeps. To Kit's ears it sounded almost like a bell, but there was a tonal quality to it that she didn't recognize.

Over the bodies on the table, two figures dressed in some sort of protective gear from head to toe worked on the bodies. They were busy injecting something into them. Under anesthetic, the bodies didn't move. The doctor edged forward and squinted harder to see details of the figures. In their garb, she couldn't make out any distinctive features. It was as if the two were wearing large, structured sacks with helmets that covered their faces and heads.

"To not let in any germs," Kit said, voice a thin breath, barely audible over the hum.

Swifty looked over at her but said nothing. He looked back down at the procedure.

The pair watched, paralyzed to act and further endanger the townspeople below. Kit recognized one of them as a frequent patron of Polly's employees—and Swifty recognized them both.

One of the victims on the table had turned gray, and the experimenters rushed over to her, moving tubes, filling them with this and that, but Kit couldn't hear what they must have been saying to each other.

She took a deep breath and concentrated on *listening*.

A whine filled her head, followed by a series of pops, clicks, and chattering—gibberish that didn't make sense at all. Searing pain pulsed through her skull, making it feel as though it would literally split. Kit reeled backward and held the sides of her head, knocking her hat onto the ground.

Swifty picked it up and put his arms around her, and at first, Kit couldn't understand who or what was grabbing her. She struggled against him, but realized it was Swifty talking to her in the distance.

The whining became even more unbearable. Her ears itched and the pressure in her head pushed against her eardrums. *Shut it off, Kathryn,* she yelled at herself, inside her own mind. *You have to shut it off.*

She imagined a dam slamming down against the flood of noise and gibbering, and all went quiet. The trickle and burn in her nose began and a flow of scarlet ran down out of her nostril and onto her lips.

"Shit, Doc, what's happening?" Swifty grabbed a handkerchief from his pocket and tried to press it to her nose, but she grabbed it from him and did it herself as she rose to her feet.

"We have to get out of here. Now." Kit ran down the narrow passageway, past the laboratory, and to the side entrance. "*Now*, Slater."

Swifty wasn't far behind, and they made it back to their ropes, jumping off the ledge and landing on the hardpan. Kit ignored her nosebleed until she landed and took her rope back, then grabbed Swifty's kerchief and used it again. The cornflower blue with the gold S embroidered on it was now mostly a dark crimson. She kept walking, as fast as her legs would stride.

"Doc, wait," Swifty collected their ropes and hooks in an attempt to leave as little a trace of themselves behind. "Wait, please—those people back there. Your nose. What in Perdition is happening?"

But Kit didn't answer him. She just kept her pace up, back toward Main Street. Swifty pursued.

"Doctor Kathryn Judge, will you please fucking answer me?" He stood in front of her and held his hands up in a stopping motion. "Please."

Kit stopped in her tracks, sniffled, and removed the kerchief from her face. The bleeding stopped but left a copper tang in the back of her throat.

"Those were experiments, Slater. *Experiments*. I don't know who they are, and I don't know why they're doing it, but I know when I see tests being run."

"So we know now—we know what's making people sick, right? We can stop them when we tell the others." Swifty still had his hands up, and Kit cocked her head.

"I'm not crazy or sick, Slater. It's just a nosebleed—so stop thinking you have to placate me or act like my caregiver." Kit put the kerchief in her pocket and waved Swifty off. "Yes, we know what's making people sick. So now what? How do we stop this? Round up a posse? Gather the town? Are you out of your fucking mind, Slater? People will either think we've gone mad, or worse: they'll believe us and try to oust those—whoever they are—and probably all get killed in the process."

"And how do you know that?" Swifty lowered his hands but put them on his hips, widening his stance.

"You saw their technology. What do you think would come of that, really? Do you think they're just here, without defenses? We don't even know where they're from—the government, or who knows." Kit stalked past Swifty and he moved before she could shoulder-check him.

"Well then what do we do, Doc?" Swifty stood there as the doctor got smaller in the distance.

"Give me time to think," Kit didn't look back as she spoke. She just stalked back to the saloon.

Swifty kicked the ground and cursed. "No. No way. I'm going back there. I'm going to figure out what to do. I can't let more people die."

But the doctor still had chaos in her head. She didn't acknowledge him. Swifty turned in the opposite direction, back to the caves.

DAYS ON END

"Doc? Doctor Judge, wake up—it's afternoon." Polly stood a fair distance from the bed, looking at the doctor. The long body of the woman that led to firm swells at the chest. Her eyes stayed there for a while then traveled to Kit's face. Polly took a step closer.

"Doc, it's two in the afternoon and your patients need you." Polly didn't touch her—she could tell from the Kit would stiffen under a hand on her arm or shoulder that it wasn't appreciated nor desired. No, this was a woman who did the touching first. After that, it might be okay. But not first.

Kit stirred and sat up stiff when she heard the word 'patients.' She looked around and up at Polly. "Oh, shit. What time is it?"

"Two o'clock, Doc. You came in so late last night, I didn't want to wake you too early. You need your sleep." She pushed the trolley forward. "I made you a Sunday brunch you can eat on your way. It's scrambled eggs and bacon in a tortilla. I put your coffee in a beer stein with a lid so you could take it with you and drink it right out of it."

Kit stared at Polly, then at the trolley, and back. The fresh coffee wafted tempting scents to the doctor. "Is this real?"

"What kind of a question is that?" Polly cocked her head. "Are you all right?" Her hand reached for the trolley again, pushing it forward by inches.

"I'm fine, don't worry." But Kit wasn't sure if this was true. She shook her head and rubbed her eyes, feeling like she had a hangover, but without any pain. Instead, she could hear with more intensity. The noises of the afternoon crowd downstairs sounded like a boisterous parade. The animals outside—horses nickering in Still's Stables and crows calling—were right in the room with her.

"Thank you, Polly. I'll take it." She picked up the breakfast tortilla and took a bite, then grabbed the stein with the other. "Guess I didn't get undressed. Even had my gun belt on. I don't remember how I got here."

"You don't remember last night, huh? Suppose I couldn't convince you we got married, then?" Polly batted her eyelashes and smiled.

Kit's face remained neutral. "No, you couldn't. That's something I'd remember, Polly, and I'd claim the honeymoon."

Polly's face turned pink. "No small feat to make me blush, Doc. But are you sure you're okay? You seem a bit off."

The doctor stood up with a grunt and made her way out the door with her hands full. "I trust you to lock up for me, Polly."

Judging by the tone of the doctor's voice, the 'do not disappoint me' was implied.

Polly didn't snoop. She understood the doctor deserved her privacy. She just made the bed, cleaned up the room, and took the trolley out, locking up like she was asked.

When Kit entered the hospital, she was greeted by three nurse's aides all rushing to give her reports of the day and what she missed. The doctor motioned for them to follow her to her office, where she hung up her duster, putting her hair into a loose bun.

"Alright, one at a time. What's wrong?"

“Well he came in this morning complaining of stomach pains. They’re mild and he’s running a low-grade fever. It’s possible he’s contaminated.”

Kit felt like someone had punched her in the stomach. “Who, Slater?”

“Yes, Doctor.”

“Get out of the way.” The doctor pushed past the nurse’s aides and took long strides to the sick ward. She threw open the door and searched the beds, finding Swifty in none of them.

“Where is he?” Kit reeled around at the aides.

“He’s in the pathology lab, and he’s locked himself inside.” Jessica was the one to answer, tranquil as the morning after a storm.

“Thanks.” Kit put her hand on the woman’s shoulder and squeezed it, then marched out of the ward.

***

Slater rested with his head on the cool mica slab, leaning his full weight onto it. The fever was starting to inch up, he could feel it, but he wasn’t going to stop until he had some answers.

Well, perhaps he'd just nap awhile. He closed his eyes and sighed. "I should've listened to the doctor. You don't listen to the doctor and that makes you dead," he said to the cool slab.

With his eyes closed, the world became a cacophony—the bustle of the hospital, the sick ward aides going back and forth, the clatter of breakfast dishes being served and then put away, the clacking of typewriters as clinical notes were neatened. The aches and pains starting in his body became dull and drifted away until he heard a key in a lock.

"Doc?"

Swifty raised his head and looked toward the door to see the tall woman with the prominent cheekbones making a sour face at him. The face softened for a moment and she closed the door behind her.

"I'm here, Slater. What's happened?"

"I may have done something kind of stupid, Doc. But I hope it was worth it." Swifty gave her a weak smile as the doctor drew close.

"Just tell me what you did—we'll fill in the rest." Kit reached up with one hand and rubbed the back of her neck.

"After we had our—our discussion last night, I thought you were wrong. So I huffed off back to the caverns and did some exploring in that laboratory of theirs. I figured eventually this is what you would've done, but I decided to do it a lot sooner."

Kit grimaced at him, arms folded across her chest. She sighed. "You're half right, Slater. But go on, anyway."

Swifty's lips curved up for a second into what might have been a grin, but the malaise was getting to him again and he sat back down on the stool, pressing his back into the counter behind him. Beads of sweat broke out on his forehead. "The lab was still empty, but they had things bubbling and brewing in there, Doc. So I put on some gloves and got some samples."

He held up three vials of a purple liquid. "Problem is, I don't know how to begin analyzing it."

"Well, I think I can help you with that, Slater," Kit said, reaching out to take one of the vials. He let it slide into her hand. His arms had weights attached to them. At some point, he stood, and tried to follow the doctor around, watching her movements as she got into her protective gear and set up the equipment.

She turned and took a long look at him, face pinching. "You're flushed. When did the symptoms start?" As she spoke, Kit set the vials down on the table in a stand. She turned and guided Swifty back to sit on the stool and leaned him against the cool countertop.

Swifty let her move him around and slouched over the lab table. "I really can't say exactly when. I went back and—it's hard to remember. I cut my hand on a rock, but I don't recall where I was. I remember being in that lab and taking the vials. I put them in my pouch in the false bottom, and then came back out into the other room. I'm hazy after that, but I remember cutting my hand."

He held out his right hand to Kit for inspection. She turned it over and looked at his palm, then the back of his hand. "I don't see a cut, Slater." Her eyes met his, and Swifty could see the concern in them. The doctor took his other hand, instead, and inspected it. She shook her head. "Are you sure you cut your hand?"

"Doc, I'm positive. After that happened, and I left the lab, I have some hazy memories. I saw faces that sort of didn't make sense. They didn't look real. I'd say they looked like a cross between a frog and a lizard with little frowning mouths and slits where noses should be. Round, black eyes like a possum. Maybe that's when the fever overtook me and I was hallucinating. I don't know, Doc. I just have a hazy memory after that and I walked back into town, went home, and slept for a couple hours."

Kit shut him up as she popped a thermometer into his mouth under his tongue and took his pulse. "Maybe you hallucinated. Maybe you didn't. There are strange things in this universe, Slater, and everything we saw *was* an experiment. I'm positive we're the subjects, but for what, I can't say."

She pulled the thermometer out of his mouth and read it. "Thirty-eight point nine four. You're starting to blaze, Slater." Putting the thermometer in the sterilizing cup, she took a bottle of aspirin from the shelf and doled out two of them. "Take these—chew them. If you need water, I'll get a nurse's aide to get you some."

Swifty shook his head and took the pills. "Don't need water. I will soon. Stomach's getting upset though. Sharp pain behind the navel—classic appendicitis symptoms but I don't have an appendix. Haven't had one since I had it out when I was ten." He sighed. "Classic whatever-this-plague-is symptoms now, I suppose."

He pointed to the vials on the shelf. "I don't want to die, Doc, but if I do, don't let it be in vain. I think that stuff might be our saving grace."

"What makes you say that?" Kit looked back to him and then to the vials.

"Because it was labeled 'palazus' which means 'antidote' in Old M'aqual."

The doctor took a deep breath, then said nothing. It came out as a long sigh.

Swifty stood and hobbled out of the room. "I'm going home, Doc. If it's an antidote, you know where to find me. But if it's not, I intend to die in my own bed."

"Wait," Kit reached out to him, but fell silent as the door shut behind Swifty with a click.

"Damn it," she said, turning back to the vials on the table. Kit sighed and put her hands on the countertop, leaning forward with her arms outstretched. "Now what?"

Silence.

Now, we work, her father's voice said in her head. It calmed the calamity of voices and worries around her.

Snapping on her gloves, Kit used a pipette to extract a small amount of liquid from the vial. “Let’s see how you interact with some abnormal tissue, shall we?”

After preparing the slide with tissue from one of the patients who died of a heart attack but was also infected, she sat back and observed through her microscope, watching the serum interact with sick tissue, ticking out the time on her pocket watch.

Time passed.

The cellular death halted.

Kit sat back and rubbed her eyes.

“This can’t be all there is to it,” she said to the vials. “There must be a trick before the treat.” The doctor stood up and exited the room as fast as she could and stopped a nurse’s aide. “David, I need you to bring me all the tissue samples from the morgue. The ones that are in the blue box in cool storage.”

“Yes, Doctor.” David stopped and turned, putting the tray of empty plates on a trolley and hurrying off to the morgue. Kit set her slides up and prepped them while she waited for David’s return.

***

Kit's stomach growled and her limbs grew heavy. She stepped out of the pathology lab and looked around. The dim lights and dark sky out the windows coupled with the smell of night blooming flowers told her that it was late.

She fished out her pocket watch and read it. "It's not late—it's early—two in the morning already." Her heart sank. "I've made so little progress."

Finding an aide named Steven in the sick ward, Kit asked him to get her a bowl of pozole and some bread from the cafeteria and bring it to her office. Thinking was becoming harder with each passing moment, and she knew that meant if she didn't take a break, her body would take a break for her. *Take a moment. Eat.* Get her head around everything that happened in the past thirty-six hours.

Steven met Kit in her office as promised and brought her the pozole, crusty bread, and a large cup of coffee. "Thanks. Could you bring me a list of patients?"

"Other than the roster?" Steven pointed to the clipboard on the wall.

"Other than. I need a list of patients who are still sick with the plague, but still lucid enough to make decisions."

She raised her eyebrows at him. "I know we're short staffed but I don't think that's too large a task."

"No, Doctor Judge. It's not. I'll get to it right away."

"Thank you." Kit turned back to her food.

Lucid patients. That would be her starting point.

Her stomach clenched as she took the first bite of food and tears stung at her eyes. *It's starting again. This is happening again.* Whispers started to drift into her head, threatening to get louder. It made her want to stop eating, curl into a ball under her desk, and die.

She forced herself to swallow the pozole and dipped her bread in the soup. The stomach pain increased, then subsided as the warm food filled her, nourished her. She drank down her bitter drink and felt the tickles of waking bubble in her head. It was enough to keep her from crashing. At least for the moment.

With her meal and coffee finished, Kit set the tray aside and put her head on her desk, letting her eyelids get heavy. She drowsed, listening, helpless to stop it.

The whispers began to fade and Kit walked down a narrow garden path, surrounded by vivid green and livid purple flowers. Smells of tobacco and jasmine filled the air, and she could hear a dog barking in the distance. A hunting hound.

She was small, feet clad in patent leather Mary Jane shoes, and her favorite white dress with tiny kittens embroidered on the front pockets, playing with balls of yarn and chasing butterflies. The girl took another step, and her foot grew, clad in bicycle boots. The doctor stopped looking at her feet and up the narrow garden path where her home loomed ahead. Father and son stood at the path, and Thomas smiled at her as the wind blew through his shaggy black hair. The baby in his arms looked around in wonder, then cooed.

When she tried to reach them again, taking another step, she was in the desert once more, clad in cowboy boots and the clothing she'd worn when she left on her journey. An eagle screamed overhead and tumbleweeds blew about in front of her. In front of her again, her husband and their baby.

She fell into a salt mine, still reaching for her son.

Something brushed her hand and she jerked upward into a sitting position. Steven stood at the other side of the desk. He had a small clipboard with him and he set it down.

"Sorry to disturb you, Doctor, but I have the list you wanted. I can take your dinner tray for you."

Kit picked up the list and nodded at him. Between the meal, the caffeine, and the catnap, she was feeling a thread of energy return. "That'll be fine. Thanks, Steven."

The nurse's aide gave her a small smile.

Alone again, Kit looked over the list of patients. She needed one of them in previous good health, sound mind, and dying.

"I can't do this. I can't ask this of them."

Kit put her face in her hands and let out a low growl. She stood up with the clipboard and paced.

"You have to, Kathryn. You must." Pace, pace, pace. She stopped herself and caught a glimpse of herself in the looking glass by the door. Her dark hair out of place, blue eyes surrounded by dark circles, and perhaps even a new wrinkle across the broad forehead. She sighed and pointed at herself. "Do the thing you cannot do."

The doctor walked to the sick ward, boots clacking with an echo that seemed too loud.

She stopped in front of the first bed on her list and looked into the eyes of a woman about her age, perhaps younger.

"You're Gemini Hsiao, yes?" Kit set the clipboard on a side table and motioned to the far end of the bed, as to ask if she could sit. Her heart thrummed in her chest as she waited to see if Hsiao would accept.

Gemini nodded and made room for the doctor to sit. "I am."

Kit sat. "How are you feeling?"

"Pretty bad. Lots of pain. Keeps me awake and the morphine doesn't put me to sleep like it does for other people. I don't know what they call it but it has the opposite effect on me." She shrugged tiny shoulders on an all-too-small frame.

"Paradoxical effect," the doctor said. "That's unusual."

"That's it, and yeah, I'm pretty unusual." The woman grinned, but it didn't last long. "I know I'm going to die, Doctor Judge. So what are you doing here? I know it's not to tell me that, at least."

"I need to talk to you about something. It's not something I want to do, actually, but I have to do something." Kit lowered her voice and leaned forward. "I have what might be an antidote. But a cure is something that takes years to find, not hours. It takes slow, dedicated research, tests on cells, then on animals, and finally, on people."

Gemini's eyes widened and she sat forward, imitating the doctor's position like a mirror image. "I understand, but how do you know it could be an antidote?"

"I did some testing on cells that were still alive, and some from the deceased," Kit said. She looked around to make sure no one was eavesdropping, and that they weren't disturbing the sleeping patients. Most were trapped in morphine dreams. "It worked on cells, but there's no way to know if it's even remotely safe in living humans. I don't want to test it on anyone, but I don't think I have a choice."

"You always have a choice, Doctor," Gemini said. She shrugged again. "Just like I do. I choose to have it tested on me."

Kit shook her head. "No. I can't do that. I can't be irresponsible with your life."

"You *aren't* irresponsible, Doctor. But you also aren't out here talking to me to ask where to find animals to test on, either. You're looking for a human because you need to see if this really is an antidote."

Kit bit her lower lip. "It was labeled as an antidote, but I'm not sure if it actually is one for humans, anyway."

"What, you think it's for dogs?"

"No—I just—it's not important." Kit waved a hand in the air, then brought it back to stroke the back of her neck.

"Tell me, Doctor. You've gone this far. Spill." Gemini's tone wasn't cruel, but firm.

Kathryn bit her lower lip, then raised her hands in surrender. "Fair enough," she said. "My conundrum is this: do I continue testing with cells, then animals, and search for other scientists to come in and help me while the whole town dies, or do I allow a person to volunteer and die anyway?"

"You know the answer to this. You're just not willing to admit it."

The two held each other's gazes, unwavering.

"No, I'm facing a real conundrum," Kit said. "This isn't simple the way you think it is. Vaccines are our best resource for preventing disease, and antidotes and 'cures' are difficult to come by, if not near impossible in many cases. Yet here I am with something that could fix this situation."

"You can't just let all these people die, and yet either way, you could kill us all." Gemini frowned. "It's not a situation I'd like to be in, Doctor."

"Yet you are," Kit said. "You could try the serum and die, or you could die anyway from the disease—or poison—whatever it is that's causing your symptoms. I can't even rightly identify it yet—a virus, bacteria, fungus, or venom. And that's the other problem. We don't know the real cause."

The two sat in silence for a moment, each caught up in their own thoughts. Kit's frustration was apparent—her frown and downcast eyes, with narrowed brows gave it away. Gemini seemed more reflective with an undisturbed brow and soft gaze.

"You can't refuse to treat a patient, can you?" Gemini cocked her head and put a finger to her lips. Kit could see little beads of sweat under her nose, breaking out on the woman's forehead.

"Well, in some ways, yes. If the patient wants me to treat them with quackery, then yes, I can refuse to give them snake oil that they think will cure them. But if someone comes to me in pain and I have the medicine to treat them, then no, I'm under ethical obligation to treat them. And I would, even if there weren't rules in place." Kit spread her hands outward, shoulders shrugging. "Why?"

"I'm asking you to treat me with what might be a cure. You have the means to treat me, Doctor Judge, so you shouldn't refuse me," the woman leaned back again and Kit could see dark circles under her eyes, rising like bruises.

The ebb and flow of deep sleep breathing from surrounding patients seemed to be lulling Gemini into sleep. Kit opened her mouth to reply but shut it again when Gemini held up a hand. "You know my request now, Doctor Judge. Think about it and decide what's more important: possibly saving lives now or waiting till the death toll is so high to introduce something that might not work either. I'll be ready in the morning. And I'll probably be worse than I am now. I don't want to die like the others. I want to live and die on my terms."

She turned over and Kit stood from the bed.

Kathryn kicked herself on the way back to the pathology lab. This was maddening. Irresponsible. She could hear whispers again and held her head. Pleas for help, past and present. People needed her to decide.

The doors to the lab closed with a quiet tick, and Kit looked around at the brilliant white walls, clean mica countertops, and her collection of supposed antidote. Her eyes stung with the frustrations of the moment and she wiped at them with a hasty hand.

“I trust you, Swifty,” she said, breathless. “And Gemini made her choice. Now it’s my turn.”

HOPE FALLS

The tall gray stones stood against a clear sky, and Gemini watched the water flow in crystal sheets as she sat beside the brook. Her great toe wiggled back and forth over a pebble stuck in the sand. She picked and picked at the smooth stone until it loosened. Once she got it rocking, her foot scooped it out and she picked it up, then examined it.

A smooth, perfectly ovular stone with pink webbing through the gray, it almost seemed to hum in her hand. Gem pressed her lips to it, feeling its satin quality against her skin. With a quiet smack, she pulled it away and dipped it into the cool river, then into her pocket.

Her feet slid into the river at the eddy, hind end planted against a worn stone that had been there since before humans ever appeared in the world. Keeping still, she watched the tiny minnows pick at her toes, feeling the tiny tickles of their mouths. She wiggled and they scattered. Still, they returned. Wiggle, scatter.

Whole body aching from the sun high above, Gemini slipped into the water the rest of the way, the coolness racing past hips, waist, and chest. Up to her neck, she went under and opened her eyes.

"Are you alright, Ms. Hsiao?" There was a fish talking to her, and Gemini shook her head. How could the trout be talking to her?

"Ms. Hsiao? Gemini?" Something brushed her shoulder.

Gem opened her eyes to see the doctor standing over her, face twisted with concern.

"I'm here. I hurt, but I'm here. I was dreaming of Hope Falls. That's where I was born." Gemini sat up on her elbows and looked at Judge. "What time is it?"

"It's seven in the morning," Judge said. She had on gloves and a syringe in her hand. "Is Hope Falls out here?"

"No, it's up in the Northwest Territory, but right on the border of North and South. I have a stone from there. I promised the stone I'd put it back someday after living a long life." Gemini frowned. "I guess that might still happen. If this works. This…" she broke off as her eyes settled on a familiar figure. "Oh no, Swifty too?"

Judge nodded. "Last night, his parents brought him in while you were asleep." She didn't say anything else. Gemini took a long look at him.

"He isn't so bad off yet, I don't think." She looked up at Judge again. "What do you think?"

"I think you should lie back and make a decision on whether or not you really want to do this. I ran some toxicity tests over the day while you slept, and I'm starting you with the smallest dose I think would work. But this is your chance to back out, Ms. Hsiao, and you can stop the test at any time." As Judge spoke, she held the capped syringe in both hands. "I'll be taking blood tests every hour, and you'll still be on intravenous fluids. We'll do everything we can to keep you comfortable and safe."

Gemini leaned into her pillows and offered her arm. "I'm ready, Doctor Judge. I want to do this because I'd rather not go the hard way."

The doctor swallowed with a soft click in her throat and uncapped the syringe, putting the needle into the tube. The royal purple fluid flooded the PICC line, coloring the clear tubing. Gemini giggled. "I feel so cool all over. It's nice."

"I'm glad it feels pleasant," Judge said, removing the needle slowly. "I'm going to do a brief saline flush, so you'll still feel cool."

Gem closed her eyes and enjoyed the sensation up her right arm. A flood of the cold entered her chest, then got warm. It felt like a blanket from the inside, somehow. She smiled. "Mm."

A cold sensation on her forehead. Her belly flip-flopped the way it did when she used to jump off the edge of the falls and into the water. She was there again, slipping into the cool water, her dog Perseus jumping in behind her and paddling with his fat paws, head above water, biting at the splashes.

She floated down the river, the dog running alongside the bank, barking his gargantuan greetings, jumping in to join her, then jumping out again. Gemini felt a gentle tug on her shoulder.

Swimming to the bank, the tall grass enveloping her in a thousand tiny hugs, the dog shaking off and getting his droplets on her. She sputtered and laughed.

"This is the day, Perseus. I'm going to put the rock back." She fished around in her pocket, then came back emptyhanded.

***

"Ms. Hsiao's vitals, Doctor—they're improving. Her fever's down without aspirin. She's more lucid than before. Able to stay on topic and fully oriented. I don't know what happened, Doctor, but what you gave her seems to be working." David handed over Gemini's chart and Kit took it from him, looking it over and scowling.

Her face softened after a moment, and she breathed a sigh that David recognized as relief. "Good. This is good. We'll see if she comes out of it overnight. Recheck her each hour, and I want her full labs. Label them with the time taken—don't forget."

"Yes, Doctor."

"I'll be in the lab. Call me for emergencies, and be sure to fetch me for rounds if I seem to forget, okay?" Kit turned on her heel and walked toward the lab as David gave her a final 'yes, Doctor.'

The remains of her lunch left behind in her office, Kit sat in the lab for a moment and sighed, closing her eyes. There, the familiar sounds of dings and the hiss of machines working blocked out most of the noise outside of the lab. If she focused on it long enough, she could block out the outside world entirely and focus on what she had in front of her. The problem.

Problem on top of problem, really—being the only doctor in the growing town was putting a strain on her, and Kit considered herself lucky to have access to the chemists. They had been instrumental in helping her figure out whether or not the serum was safe to use on humans. She didn't tell them where she found it, and let them believe she had concocted it herself—they'd think she was insane if she explained. After that, she let them analyze it. They pronounced it safe and that they didn't see any problems with it—that it looked like such-and-such a compound.

Fine. It could've been fructose and cocaine with coagulants at that point—did it work and was it safe were her only questions. If they didn't recognize anything dangerous, well, she trusted them. Larson Ikechukwu was an expert in his field, and she might have taken chemistry for her medical degree, and understood it well enough, but she wasn't a pharmacist. They were the true experts when it came to medicines and curatives. She trusted him and his colleague, Kenneth Rodriguez.

A knock at the door brought Kit from her woolgathering and she unlocked it, opening it a crack. "Doctor?"

It was a short, red-haired woman who looked like she might blow away in a strong wind. She was holding an envelope with something in it.

"Yes, what is it?" Kit extended her hand to take the envelope. The young woman pushed it into her hands.

"It's for you. Gemini asked me to give this to you before she fell asleep."

Kit turned the envelope over in her hands. "Um, wait just a moment."

She opened the envelope an extracted a piece of paper, clutching the bulge in the envelope with one hand while unfolding the paper with the other.

Dear Doctor Judge,

Thank you for giving me a chance to live. I don't know if I'll make it, but I'm starting to feel better. Yet I'm still not sure if I'm recovering yet, as I still have a lot of stomach pain and am weak.

I have a favor to ask of you. My family won't understand this, but I think you might.

If I don't survive, please take this rock back to Hope Falls with you someday. It doesn't have to be right away, but I made a promise, and though it's just a rock, I always keep a promise. That rock belongs in my hometown, not here in this dry and unforgiving climate. It's a river rock, and deserves to be home.

So please. Take it home and drop it on the East Bank of the Hope Falls cliffs. When you see my home, you'll understand why.

Thank you for giving me one last chance.

With friendship,

Gemini Hsiao

Kit nodded and brushed by the nurse's aide, going to her office and putting the envelope and letter in her duster's inside pocket. She stood in front of the coatrack, extending one hand to lean on the wall in front of her. If she were a cultist, it would look like she was praying, with her eyes closed and the room encased in silence. The doctor didn't pray. She centered herself.

When she emerged from her entombment, she walked back into the sick ward. Gemini was sleeping, so Kit pulled out her notepad and a pen from her lab coat.

Dear Ms. Hsiao,

I promise.

With friendship,

Kathryn Judge, MD

She pressed the note into Gemini's hand with a gentle touch, and ducked out of the room so as not to wake her patient from the much-needed rest. Long strides carried her back to the lab, and once again, she was alone.

The doctor began her work of analyzing her patient's blood. Hsiao, Gemini; female; age 33. Kit felt a hitch in her chest and brought her hand to her heart. The locket and vial clinked as she put her hand there. She swallowed and closed her eyes, taking a deep breath to still the cramp in her muscle.

Relieved, she went back to work, and David came by to bring her more samples of Hsiao's blood.

She couldn't see the serum at work, but she could see its effects. Her red cell count had risen back to normal levels. Low normal, but still, it was better than before. "That explains your weakness."

Preparing another slide, she checked that one next. A slight increase. Good. But not good enough.

After checking three more slides, Kit went to grab a fourth when the bell in the sick ward chimed, indicating an emergent situation. The doctor jumped up from her seat and hurried out the door, making it into the sick ward in a matter of seconds.

"What happened?" Kit came forward to see three aides crowding around Gemini's bed and pushed two of them out of her way.

"She sat up, read something, said her chest hurt and stopped breathing."

Kit put her stethoscope to Gem's chest and listened. The woman's pulse was faint.

"I'm starting resuscitative measures. David give me one cc epinephrine through IV push. Go."

"I don't know how," David said. "I'm still working on it."

"Fuck," Kit grabbed the syringe from his hand and uncapped it, doing the IV push herself. She bent down over Gemini and sealed the woman's nose with her fingers, tilting her chin up and back, then pressing her lips over Gem's to form a seal. She exhaled into her patient's mouth, then turned her head to listen.

The sound of a gurgle caused Kit to lurch back as Gemini spewed a flood of blood from her body. Though it wasn't projectile, it flowed like a waterfall from her mouth and onto the bed, her body, and the floor.

"No. Please, no," Kit put her hand on Gemini's wrist, put her stethoscope to the woman's chest, and shook her head. She started chest compressions. Nothing.

Minutes passed. Hsiao didn't respond. Kit tried again. Still nothing.

She held onto the woman's wrist, feeling for a pulse. She watched her pocket watch as two minutes ticked by. "I'm calling it. Time of death is eighteen-thirty-seven."

When she took her hand away, she left a smear of blood behind, and it spread to her lab coat. The doctor's jaw set and her eyes narrowed. She felt as though she'd run ten miles with a full pack. "Clean up, please, and get blood and tissue samples. I'll notify the family and perform an autopsy immediately."

Kit left the room to do her job, grimacing, face pale. She went to the washroom and cleaned her hands until they were bright red from scrubbing, then tossed her lab coat into the laundry. It landed with a rustle.

After that, she went back to the sink and washed her face. Anything to keep herself steady.

***

"Given the evidence in front of me, the cause of death for this patient was hypovolemic shock brought on by gastrointestinal hemorrhage. Report is made by Kathryn Judge, MD, Acting Coroner for the town of Platt's Gulch." Kit pressed the stop pedal with her foot and snapped off her gloves.

"Jessica, you can close and take her to viewing. Have her family collect her and all that. You know what to do, right?"

"Yes, Doctor. You tried. You made her last day in the world a lot better."

Kit shook her head and clenched her teeth. "It wasn't enough."

Jessica looked like she might say something, but kept silent and started closing the body.

"I'm going to Polly's and getting some rest. Hold down the fort for me. Comfort measures only."

She didn't give the aide a chance to reply. The doctor left the morgue and back up to her office. Trudging forward, she put on her duster and headed out the door, not saying a word to anyone.

When she swung open the doors to Polly's, she got the usual stares and did her best to shut down the whispers that tried to evade her mental blockades. As people resumed their activities, Kit sat down in the place that had become 'the Doc's spot' in the corner across from the bar. A booth that enabled the doctor to have her back against the wall and look out at everyone incoming and egressing. She stretched out one leg on the rest of the bench and motioned Polly over once she caught the blonde's eye.

"Two bottles of whiskey, one glass. I've got a two-bottle problem," Kit pulled out two gold pieces from her pouch and set them down on the counter. "This should cover the expenses you've been racking up for me, Pol."

Polly's eyes widened and she picked up the gold pieces, turning away to bite the soft metal and check them. When she turned back, her eyes were still as wide and disbelieving as they'd been when she first saw the nuggets. "It'll cover it and then some. You sure about this?"

"The gold, or the whiskey?" Kit looked up at Polly, scowling. "Because I'm sure about both. So please, back off. I'm fucking tired, Polly. Don't give me shit and bicker like a goddamn fishwife."

Polly looked like Kit kicked her in the groin, and Kit held up her hand. "No, Polly, I'm so sorry. It's just a bad day, and I don't want to take it out on you. Forgive my transgression. Just give me the whiskey and steer clear of me."

The well-curved blonde nodded and walked away, and Kit put her hand to her eyes, pinching above the bridge of her nose, between her eyebrows. The crowd noise was soothing in its way, as long as it stayed on the outside. It ebbed and flowed like a river in a rainstorm, swelling when the rain worsened, then to a lull when the sprinkles came.

Clang, clang, tap.

Kit opened her eyes to see two large bottles of whiskey and a shot glass in front of her. "Here, Doc. Your whiskey and your glass. I'll be back if you need anything." Polly's tone wasn't cold like Kit expected from that rebuff. Instead, she was gentle, the way a person handled a horse when the filly was wild and had to be caught. Roping them worked for some, sure, but good handlers knew the best way was to be gentle and befriend.

"Thanks, Polly," she said, and put her head back on the back of the booth's seat.

"I'm here if you want to talk," she said.

Polly left at a slow walk, and Kit poured her first shot, knocking it back and letting the burn cut her tongue, numb her lips, and tingle in her ears. Her eyes watered, and she poured herself another glass. This time, it didn't burn as much.

About halfway through the second bottle, Kit discovered her legs were missing and then discovered she didn't give a damn. She looked toward the door to see the tiny Yaja enter the Saloon with the deputy, Yina, right behind her. They were talking and animated, then went to the bar to see Polly. Kit took another drink.

Money and food exchanged hands and Kit watched the corn with fascination. "Corn is a grass," she said to the empty bottle. "Did you know that?"

The bottle (mercifully) did not respond. She knocked it over with a flick of her finger.

"And you're dead. Just like that. One minute you're here, full of promise, potential. Then next? Boom. Dead as a fucking signpost." Kit leaned back and her hair fell over her eyes. She pulled her one outstretched leg up and resting it against the back of the booth. It still didn't feel much of anything.

She wasn't going to tear up over this. Patients died every day. That's what people did. Crying about it wasn't going to help them, and it wasn't going to help her now.

Footsteps came closer and Kit put her hand on the butt of her revolver, "I might be drunk but I'm not so drunk I can't aim," she said.

"No, Doc, no trouble." Yaja's voice had a laugh in it. Kit tipped her hat back up to see Yaja and Yina standing there.

"Oh for shit's sake, can't you tell when someone wants to be alone?" Kit poured herself another shot and tipped it back, hat falling back off her head as she drank.

"Yes, but you *don't* want to be alone. If you wanted to be alone, Doctor Kit, you'd be holed up in your room with your bottles. No, you're here for company." Yaja sat down and Yina joined her, both across from Kit. Yaja turned to face the bar. "Polly? Can you bring over another bottle?"

Polly reached under the counter and came up with one in each hand, and shot glasses. She put them all on a tray and meandered her way to the doctor's table.

Kit grumbled about wanting to be left alone again, but Yaja ignored her. Yina looked concerned, frowning.

"Seems like it's been a long day for our doctor," Polly said as she opened the bottle. She poured out the shots and looked over at Kit, then sat down in the booth next to her. "Come on, long and lean—what happened to you today?"

"History. History happened to me today. I'll go down in history as the shittiest doctor ever, and I don't care. Not about that. I care that I couldn't save Gemini today. That no matter what I do, they keep dying. Oh sure, it's what people do, we can't change that end result, I get it. But I can't just sit there and let it happen." Kit poured herself another drink and ran her hand through her hair. "Problem is, I've been through this before."

The three others turned their attention to Kit—Polly and Yina grave, Yaja's face kind and expectant. Kit found something akin to comfort in that face. Not just comfort, but courage. The courage to speak. To say the words that she never wanted to speak aloud. To speak aloud was to make it true.

"I killed my son."

THE KILLER'S HAND

1901: Charles Town, Southeast Territory. A boy played in the white sands, collecting sand dollars and bringing them to his mother. "You think these were ever really worth something, Mama?"

Kit laughed. "You're almost a man now, Thomas. You tell me. Why do you think they're called 'sand dollars,' then?"

Thomas coughed, then shrugged. "Figure because they're shaped like coins, and whatever lived in them must have thought they were worth something."

Kit nodded. "Good. Sand dollars are echinoid, burrowing sea urchins. What you're holding is a skeleton of one that's washed ashore. Something didn't live in them, they were them. All that's left is the dry 'bone.' You understand?"

The boy with the big blue eyes looked up at his mother and nodded. "This was a big one. I bet he thought he was worth a lot. Or it, I mean."

The doctor reached out and ruffled his hair. "Do you think it thinks the way we do?"

Thomas shook his head. "Not really, but maybe they do. Our brains are different and theirs isn't like ours, but their experience might be similar." He thought about it a moment, then shook his head. "I think it's bad if we don't give other animals a chance, though. If we put them down and say they aren't as good as us, that leads to people abusing them." He coughed again and Kit put her hand on his back.

"I don't think the moist air is helping. Let's get you inside and get warm. We'll get Priscilla to make you a chicken soup and crusty bread for dinner. What do you think about that?" She put her hand to his forehead, then led him inside.

"I'm pretty hungry," he said, trying not to lean in too close to his mother.

Though Thomas ate his soup and bread with the gusto afforded those young boys who were about to go through a growth spurt. Kit rubbed eucalyptus oil on his chest and tucked him in—all while trying to pretend she wasn't tucking him in.

"It's pretty bad, isn't it?" Thomas asked, eyes half-closed.

"I'm sure you'll be better soon," she said, masking the concern in her voice. "Just sleep, sweetheart. Rest is often the best thing for an illness like this."

He didn't answer.

The next morning, his cough was worse and his sputum was green—a thick, spongy mucus all over the front of his night shirt. Kit and Priscilla helped him change into a fresh one, and Kit listened to his lungs.

She shook her head. "He's got it, too, and he's not recovering. This illness is worse than the Great Plague, I swear."

"But shouldn't Thomas have your immunity?" Priscilla stirred an antipyretic powder into some water and let it dissolve.

"No, it doesn't work that way. I'm not still breastfeeding my eleven-year-old. What we need is the cure, but since the blockade, those ships aren't coming in with it, so we're stuck. I mean, we've been rationing for weeks anyway." She clenched her fists. "I hate politics."

Priscilla put her hand on Kit's shoulder and squeezed it. "Couldn't you just make some? You said last week the formula was simple and it'd only need to incubate a few days."

Kit bobbled her head slightly and appeared to mull it over. "I'd need a sample. You wouldn't happen to have a sample, would you?"

The governess grinned. "No, of course not, but I might know someone who could get me some. You'd just have to, you know, defy the Union government, use the hospital for nefarious purposes, and start saving lives." Here, she turned serious. "I don't mean to be flippant—and please take this with kindness—you know only two percent of people who get this illness survive without treatment. Chances are Thomas is going to die when the plague runs its course."

Kit paled, chewing on her lips. "I know, and I have to do something. I can't just sit here and let all these people die. I need that sample, Pris. Can you really get it for me?"

"The less you know, my friend, the better, but I'll say this: I have a friend on the inside where the samples are kept. I won't leave empty-handed."

The doctor put her hand on Priscilla's and gave it a squeeze. "I don't pay you enough."

Priscilla laughed. “Maybe you should come to my room at night, pay me with nature’s tender.”

“Harassment. You always harass me, Pris.” Kit chuckled despite her dark mood. “You know I’d never do that, right?”

“I know. That’s why I’m here. I get to tease you constantly and get away with it.”

Kit nodded. Her face had fallen again, heavy with concern. “This has to work. I have to do this.”

“I’ll bring you the sample tonight, more if I can get it.” Priscilla headed for the door, then turned back. “I could get a crate.”

Kit shook her head and gestured for emphasis. “No. We can’t have anything traced back here. Just enough that they won’t notice is missing until everyone’s healthy again. Then they can arrest me, hang me for sedition. I don’t care. I have to do what’s right, and that’s at cross-purposes with what’s legal right now.”

Priscilla opened the door and gave the doctor a long look. “Isn’t it always that way?”

Kit sniffed. “Mostly.”

The door made a gentle click as Priscilla closed it. Kit opened up the windows to let in the breeze.

***

"I've got it, Pris. It took me a week, but if we put this in the water or in the food, people will start recovering within twenty-four hours. Takes a little longer than the intravenous injection, but that shouldn't be a problem." Kit held a tray full of vials. "Make sure you put one vial for each gallon of soup, and make sure that only those who are sick get it."

Priscilla took one of the vials from her and examined the puce liquid inside. "Looks like a perfume sample."

"Don't put it behind your ears. I'm serious about not giving it to the well. People who don't need it often wind up immune to its effects if they need it later, so we might be better off putting a tenth of it in each tray." Kit looked up from her work. "How is Thomas doing?"

"Thomas is hanging on this morning. His cough's still bad though, and there's a rattle in his chest I don't like." She turned the vial all around up against the light as she spoke, fascinated with the medicine inside.

“How many are still at the hospital?” The doctor looked in the direction of Thomas’s room as she asked the question.

“Thirty-six still living—not one of them is slated to recover.”

Kit put her hand over her chest and closed her eyes for a moment. “Those poor people,” she said, voice a hard whisper. “We have enough for all of them, thankfully. It’d be another week for me to make more, and they’d all be dead by then.”

Priscilla put the vial back on the tray. “So one-tenth of a vial for each of them?”

Kit nodded. “For adults. That’s only half for the children under 45 kilograms. This stuff is difficult to overdose, but I don’t want to risk it.”

“I’ll get Cherry to help me distribute it. She works in the infirmary and she’s aggravated at the blockade. Probably all those medicines are wasted now.”

“Thank you, Pris. And they probably are—without the coolers, they don’t have a long shelf life. Only about three or four days.”

Priscilla took the tray of vials. "I'll put these in a box under a couple of blankets we can bring in for the patients. The nights are so cold on the water. So you'll be a double-hero."

Kit felt heat come into her cheeks and she waved her hand at Priscilla. "I don't want to be a hero, Silla. I just want this damn disease to stop killing people, and I want our government to stop being so incredibly stupid."

"Well you ask for too much. Diseases come and go, but the government is stupid forever." Priscilla found a box and put in egg crates, then laid the vial holder on top of that, tucking it in tight enough so the glass didn't move.

"Maybe so. Hand me one of those vials. I'm going to give Thomas his dosage." Kit's outstretched hand made a grab motion.

Priscilla took out one of the vials and handed it to the doctor. Kit took it from her and removed the seal with a soft popping sound. The doctor measured out the contents to exactly a fifth, then put the seal back on and set it aside.

"I'll put that in the incinerator later. Be careful how you dispose of everything—it really shouldn't get in the ground water, so burning is our only option." Kit stirred Thomas's orange juice and added a pinch of sugar to it, then stirred that in as well.

"Don't worry, Kit, I'll take care of this." Priscilla grabbed the box and left the kitchen, out to the linen closet. She picked three blankets and stuffed them into the box with care, ensuring they didn't crush the glass vials. "But I think I'll take a dose when I'm at the hospital. I'm getting the cough, myself."

"Take it with food so it won't upset your stomach," the doctor said. She looked at her friend and nurse with concern. "Is it a bad cough?"

"Not yet. Stop worrying about me." Priscilla waved her off and kept walking. Kit took the tray of food and a powder upstairs to Thomas's room.

She found her son asleep in an upright position, head leaning back against his soft pillows and snoring through his open mouth, dying light of the sun casting pink and gold throughout the room. Using her elbow, she flicked on the light switch and a soft glow chased the fiery colors away, awash in white light.

"Thomas, wake up and eat your dinner."

The boy stirred at the sound of his mother's voice and opened his eyes partway. "I'm not hungry, Mama."

"That's fine, but I need you to drink your juice. I put your medicine in it and there isn't much of it, but you need your fluids. It'll help keep your fever down, too."

Thomas tried to sit up more and coughed—a wet sound from deep in his chest. Kit winced.

"Can you breathe?" She watched her son's face turn red as he wheezed. He nodded.

"Yeah, it's just hard to cough, though."

"I know it is, but the juice will put a stop to all that. It'll take you a few days to recover but you'll feel so much better come morning you might even get out of bed." Kit smiled and put the tray over his lap. "Do you need help?"

The boy shook his head. "No, I'm almost a man now. I can do it," he propped himself up on his elbows and sniffed. "Will the juice make me throw up?"

"I don't think so. If you feel like you will I can give you an antiemetic. That'll help you keep it down. Have you been vomiting, Thomas?" Kit tried not to sit forward or lean in too close. She leaned in a little, but not enough to irritate her son.

"No. I just cough so much I feel like I might." Thomas shrugged and took the juice. "I just want to feel better."

"I know. Drink up, then. It's not a lot of juice and the medicine might be a little bitter, but I put some sugar in to help." Kit forced herself to sit back and let Thomas take care of himself.

He drank the juice in three long gulps and set down the glass, then coughed. His exhale made the rattling that Priscilla described, and the doctor winced again.

"Mama?"

"What is it?"

"Can you show me a magic trick?" Thomas opened his eyes. "That always makes me feel better."

Kit nodded, using sleight-of-hand to extract a coin from her dress pocket. She snapped her fingers and the coin appeared on Thomas's plate. "Well now, how did that get there?"

Her son giggled and picked up the coin. "I like President Carver quarters."

"Well, would you like to keep it?" Kit asked, outstretching one hand.

"Yes, please."

Kit took the coin from him. "So to keep it, you'll have to find it," she said, using her hands to simultaneously distract and hide the coin. "I'll give you three guesses."

Thomas pointed to his plate. "Under."

Kit picked up the plate. "No, guess again."

The boy grinned. "Is it in my ear again?"

His mother made a grand investigation. "No, goodness. Where did that coin go?"

Thomas looked around and shrugged. "I don't know, Mama. Is it in your ear?"

Kit laughed and snuck the coin to her ear, then lifted her hair for her son to see. "I thought I felt some pressure."

The boy giggled and took the coin, putting it on his side table. "I think I'll eat my soup later. Will you sit with me awhile?" Thomas reclined and closed his eyes. Stillness settled over the room and Kit sat back, taking in her son's features. She tried to act as if she wasn't looking at him, keeping busy with the comforter.

Thomas opened his eyes and stared at his mother. "Do I look like Papa?"

The abrupt question gave Kit a start, and she looked up from picking lint off the bed. She cocked her head and gave

Thomas a long look. "You do. You're a good mix of me and of your father. I see his cheekbones when I look at you, and I see his chin. You have his lips, too. I think when you grow up, you'll look a lot more like him, but with my nose and my eyes."

One corner of Thomas's mouth turned up in a smile, but he didn't say anything. The room grew ever silent, with just the sound of breathing and a wheeze, the ocean pounding the shore in the distance, and the calls of night birds singing to the sunset.

When the sun dipped below the horizon, Kit shut off the lights and took Thomas's tray, setting it aside on the service table. She rested at the foot of the bed.

Closing her eyes, Kit fought sleep through heavy lids and when she opened them again, moonlight from a full, fat moon lit the room in silver streams. The doctor sat up and turned on the lights, taking her stethoscope and thermometer from the drawer. She turned to her son and warmed the diaphragm against her hand so as not to wake him.

She pressed the chest-piece to Thomas's chest and listened.

He wasn't soundly asleep. There was no sound at all. No heartbeat. No lung sounds. Nothing.

The only heartbeat was her own, pounding in her ears as her legs went weak and knees filled with water.

"No. Thomas, no, please!" Kit began chest compressions and her hands touched his frozen skin. She let out an ear piercing scream and ran out the door.

"Silla—Priscilla, where are you?"

No answer. Kit ran down the stairs, still calling for Priscilla. The house was silent.

Silent, except for her wails, then the crashing of glass as she threw a silver tray into a curio cabinet.

Still screaming (NOT MY SON!) dazed, and seeing nothing but red, Kit grabbed the cabinet and pulled it as hard as she could. It tipped and fell forward, hitting the marble floor. The china inside crashed and tinkled as they broke. The doctor walked across the shards and sherds on bare feet, the cuts not registering as she fell to her knees and tore at her clothes. She screamed her son's name until she was hoarse.

OUT OF SILENCE

"That's it. The next day, when I found out they had all died, I realized it wasn't a fluke—that it was my actions that killed them. They blamed the illness mixed with bad food, and said Thomas died of the illness. I buried my son with the seed of an oak at Judge Manor, and left everything to Priscilla's family that remained. I started walking. I was nothing better than a murderer, and now—it's happening all over again." Kit swiped the bottle off the table and emptied it into her shot glass, knocking the last one back as quickly as she had the first.

"It was my fault. I don't know if the sample was tainted and I incubated a bad batch, or if I was just far out of my league. Whatever it was, it doesn't matter, because my hubris brought me here, and I'm not about to be this foolish again. Gemini died because of that serum, and Thomas died because of my serum."

The three women with Kit sat in silence for what seemed like hours. Polly's face was streaked with tears. Yina held back tears, and Yaja looked as though she'd been punched in the stomach.

"It wasn't your fault," Yina said after the silence threatened to break them. "You couldn't have known the sample was bad, and I'm sure you weren't out of your league."

"I'm a pathologist, but I shouldn't have done it alone. It's not a single genius that makes leaps in science, or even a single individual of average intelligence. It's a team of researchers over a lifetime of painstaking work, and it's the process, not the individual, that makes the science sound. In my rush to save people, I set that aside." Kit's sweat mingled with her tears and she wiped at her face. "Intentional or not, no matter. This is my lot and I have to face it. I can't do the same thing here."

"Kathryn, stop it," Yaja said. "There are sick people and there will always be sick people. Doctors treat them. Sometimes the treatment goes wrong. People are allergic, or their bodies can't handle it. You didn't do this on purpose. Until you face what you did in the past and let it go, you will repeat the same mistakes. You have the chance to face it now—and you are by telling us this, so stop making it about you and your failures and start focusing on what it's really about: saving people through the process of science. Focus on what you need to do next."

Polly reached out and put her hand over Kit's. Kit didn't take it away. Polly gave it a squeeze. "I think you need to listen to Yina and Yaja. You didn't murder your son. If he'd died with you doing nothing, you think you'd feel any less guilty?"

The doctor swallowed and shrugged. "Probably not."

"Focus on what's in front of you, Kathryn," Yina said. "What serum did you develop?"

"You're all going to think I'm over the cliff with this one—I—I didn't develop it." Kit rubbed the back of her neck and took a deep breath. "Slater found it."

"What do you mean, he 'found' it?" Yaja asked. She took a drink from her shot glass and set it aside.

"Well, I mean we went searching after that glow in the foothills—in the caverns, and we found something extraordinary. It was—and you're going to think I'm insane but I'm not—it was a laboratory. Never seen one like it before. The technology was far beyond anything I'd encountered even during my studies in Albion."

Yina raised her eyebrows, and Polly shrugged, eyes wide. Yaja, however, didn't lose her expression of gentle curiosity.

"The M'aqual have known for generations that the caverns are Harvester Territory, I don't see why you two are acting surprised. Those stories came from somewhere, you know. Real encounters. Not dreams. Not always dreams." Yaja shrugged. "So you found the Harvesters."

"I don't know what I found, Yaja—it may be your Harvesters, or it may be something the government has set up around here. It could be anything. I don't have enough information. But Slater got sick, I was working alone, and I checked that serum with the pharmacists. They couldn't find anything harmful in it, so who knows. The gastrointestinal hemorrhage could have been developing despite treatment. None of it matters, I'm back at the beginning and I need a team out here to help me." Kit put her head in her hands. "So that's it. I don't know what else to do except heave up this alcohol and go to bed."

Yina's face had gone from sympathetic to alarmed, as if the doctor had gone mad, but now, she just looked exhausted and she reached out to pat Kit on the arm. "The

Harvesters. I'd never heard that one before, but whatever you encountered, I'm sure we'll figure it out. For now, though, we should keep this to ourselves. I don't want to start a panic."

Kit took Yina's hands in both of hers. "That's exactly what I think, too. But are you alright, Yina? You look pained."

The woman nodded. "Just a headache. From the alcohol. Diribe always makes fun of me for not being able to drink. I'll be fine come morning. I have aspirin gum and live right near the river for water. Best thing to kill headaches is a morning swim."

She leaned forward and kissed Kit on the forehead, and Kit leaned into her, comforted. "You get some sleep, Doc. I'm heading home. Yaja, you coming?"

Yaja shrugged. "Might as well. Gotta get up to trade tomorrow at the M'aqual Post." She stood up and clapped Kit's shoulder. "Your past is not your future, but they're connected. You're a good person, Kathryn, whether you believe it or not."

"Thank you, Yaja," Kit's words were slurred, and she looked up at the woman with shining eyes. "I don't believe it, but I appreciate it."

Polly put her arm around Kit. "Come on, old girl. I'm taking you upstairs and putting you to bed."

"Not before I heave," the doctor wobbled on her legs and Polly gripped her waist tighter to steady the tall woman.

"Newborn foals walk about as well," Polly said. "Come on, sweet Doctor, let's get upstairs."

She guided her back to her room, taking her into the water closet.

"It's not right, Polly. I should have been the one to die, not him," Kit said between heaves into the bowl. Polly handed her a cold washcloth. The doctor wiped her mouth.

"I know you think that way, any mother might think that."

Doctor Judge didn't reply. She got up and made it into her bed, face down. Polly took her gun belt off her, keeping it on the table nearer too the door, then took care to get her out of her clothes and into a nightshirt. Kit didn't move.

***

The crack of thunder and flash of lightning that came with it woke Kit from her dead sleep. She looked around, down to her nightshirt, and back up again. Alone. The weight of the night still on her shoulders, but clearheaded. She'd wretched up the poison.

She sat up and put her feet on the floor, holding her head in her hands. She'd cried as much as she ever did when she was drunk, and her eyes were dry, making sticky clicking sounds when she blinked. Kit slouched and put her head between her knees, looking under the bed for her boots.

Polly had folded her clothing neatly and left her shoes under the bed at the foot. She reached out for them and another flash of lightning surged, followed by a thunderclap two seconds later. The storm was passing.

She stood up and went to the water closet, then washed her face to unstick her eyes.

The past and the future.

It was part of what Yaja said to her earlier. It made it through the haze, but there was more to it. Something that Kit couldn't hear in her drunken fog.

There was a whisper along with it.

Those whispers had been with the doctor ever since she was a child. The things she could hear and knew before anyone else knew them. The whispers that made learning so easy and understanding people so hard. They said one thing, whispered another. She'd learned to accept that about them, because she was often that way, herself.

You tie it together, Kathryn. Your past, your present. You define these things, and you have the answers.

That whisper that came from Yaja when she said good night came to her as though she hadn't heard it before. But it gave her an idea.

The vial around her neck clinked, and the doctor dried off her face, tossing the soiled towel into the hamper. "I have the answers. My past. My present. Their future."

Kit dressed between flashes of lightning and headed out the door.

INCUBATION

"This is what I was missing," Kit said to the chemist. "Here, have a look at this. Tell me if it's safe. If you think it'll work."

Rodriguez took the sample from her and had a look in it in the brightly lit pathology lab. He made himself comfortable on the stool as he waited for the slide to gel before inserting it. "I was surprised the first antidote didn't work, but maybe we were all overlooking something." He looked from the slide back up to Kit. "How long have you been working on this one?"

"Ten days. It had to incubate for three and I've been using tissue and animal tests. So far, only one death." Kit shrugged. "I need more time, really, and more people. More process."

Rodriguez shook his head. "We don't have that luxury out here, Doctor Judge. Mostly we have to come up with antidotes and more just on the edge. It's not great but we do with what we have."

"Do you ever remedy anything?" Kit raised an eyebrow at him.

"We do. Found a method to prevent kidney stones, both oxalate and calcium. You may have heard of it—Opsirate in a magnesium solution. That was invented out here when Griselda Alvarez almost lost her mother to sepsis from a duct blockage. Doctor Alvarez found that in a month, and now it's a staple worldwide." Rodriguez shrugged. "Necessity's the forefather of invention, right?"

Kit nodded. "I suppose so." She inclined her head towards the slides and power scope. Her legs ached and she stood up for a moment, stretching.

"Whatever happened to Doctor Alvarez?" The doctor looked around as though she might be hiding in the corner.

"She was one of the first to die. Sad." Rodriguez shook his head. "At first we thought it must have been contagious because of that."

The doctor put her hands in her back pockets and rolled her shoulders. "She worked here with Harlan. No one mentioned that."

"She did. One of the few doctors who stayed behind, just counted among the other dead, I suppose."

"As so often happens in an epidemic." Kit frowned. "So, what do you think of the new concoction, then?"

"Let's take a look," he turned back to his studies. He was quiet for a long time and Kit observed him observing the serum. She sat back on the stool again and held her hands in her lap as Rodriguez did his work, making notes along the way.

"This might be one that gets used worldwide if this plague starts to spread, Doctor Judge." The large man pushed his stool back and the scraping noise echoed in the lab. "I think you can test it on some of your more severe subjects, and it should be safe. I know that's what Ikechukwu said last time, but there's nothing in this that would harm a human, especially if your other tests were safe. But I'll stake my reputation on it. It's worth trying."

"Thanks, Kenneth. Take a laurel out of petty cash." Kit put her hand to her heart and raised it to her side again. "Thank you."

Rodriguez returned the gesture and headed out of the room. "Come by the pharmacy sometime and we'll talk shop. I'd love you to meet my family."

The corners of Kit's mouth twitched into what could have been a smile (it didn't last long), and she nodded. "I'd like that. If I get a chance, I will."

When Kit was alone once more, she collected her samples for the cooler, and went out to see if she could get a volunteer.

She's getting too close.

Kit stopped in the hallway and looked around. The whisper in her head seemed loud, as if someone had been standing behind her and gave a stage whisper. But no one was in the hall with her. She only heard people in the sick ward, and the cafeteria.

With a scowl, she took a deep breath and tried to 'feel' with her mind to hear who was telling her that she was getting too close. The tendrils, or feelers that she put out around her, coiled like impossibly long snakes, then turned back empty. That deepened her scowl. She stopped, shook her head, and took another deep breath. At least she saved herself from a nosebleed this time. Back to the sick ward.

Nearest to the door lay a young man in his twenties, hooked up to intravenous fluids, medicines, and an oxygen mask over his nose and mouth. Kit's expression softened from its usual sculpture-in-stone to a face that was far more maternal. "Slater? How are you doing?

Swifty opened his eyes and gave Kit a weak wave, moving his fingers inches off the mattress. "I keep telling the Taker to piss off—I'm not finished yet." He drew in a deep breath through his mask. "Any luck putting together a team?"

"A bit," Kit pulled up a chair and sat close. "Rodriguez and I have been going back and forth with a little something based of one of my old potables." She leaned in close and lowered her voice. "Some time back I made a serum that didn't work. At first, I thought it was tainted. It isn't. Now I think I know what went wrong, and I've fixed the problem. I need a volunteer to test it, though, and I'm not sure if I should do this again or not. Not after what happened with Ms. Hsiao."

Swifty didn't sit up, but he looked at her with bright interest through dull eyes. "Tell me what to do, Doc. I'll volunteer."

Kit explained the testing process and everything that she and Rodriguez had discussed, then sat back and let Swifty mull it over. He gave her a weak smile. "I'm in for it. Sounds like a risk I need to take soon, or else."

"I won't lie to you, Slater—this might not do anything, but I need to take you off all other medicine while you take this. No aspirin, nothing. Just IV fluids and J003." Kit spread her hands. "No trade name for the serum yet, so that's its moniker."

"Let's do it, Doc. Right now. The next time the Taker shows, I might not be able to turn them away." Swifty closed his eyes and drew in a deep breath. "Been trying not to cough, but can't hold out for long on that, either."

Kit leaned forward and ruffled Swifty's hair. "Alright, then, Slater. I'll be back in a horse's gallop."

The doctor wasted no time getting to the lab and filling a syringe with J003, and told Jessica to take Slater off all medicines and do a saline flush. Once she had everything in order, and she was sure that the aide had followed her orders, she marched back to the sick ward with a stride she hadn't had in weeks. The whisper from earlier seemed to inject her with a new fever for solving the problem before her, and she didn't fear the outcome. She accepted it.

Swifty opened his eyes as soon as Kit drew near his bed. He looked up at her and smiled through his mask. "I'm ready, Doc. Let's do this."

Kit looked to ensure the only thing he was hooked up to were his IV fluids, and then pushed the needle into his port. Swifty winced. “Damn, Doc, that burns. But it’s fine—hopefully it’ll burn this shit right outta me.”

“Let’s hope,” the doctor emptied the syringe and tossed it aside, then took his pulse. “Rock steady, Slater. You’re in good shape for a sick man.”

Swifty gave her a thumbs up gesture. “Thanks, Doc. Would you stay with me awhile? I’d like to have the company.”

“Of course I will. How about till you fall asleep?” Kit took a seat in the chair she’d been using and put the syringe and needle in the bin for sterilization.

“How about it?” Swifty made a small coughing sound, then swallowed. “You wouldn’t happen to have a moistener, would you?”

Kit felt her pockets. “I think I have a tube somewhere.” She extracted one little mouth moistener tube from her coat and moved Swifty’s mask to the side. “These masks make you dry out. Here, open.”

The young man opened his mouth and Kit put a stream of the gel in and around the edges of his mouth. "Try that. If you need more, tell me."

Swifty ran his tongue around his mouth, then nodded. Kit added another strip to his lips and along the edge of his teeth.

"Better, Doc, thanks." Swifty put his own mask back on and held up his hand. "Could I hang onto the tube?"

"Sure. Here you go." Kit put it in his hand and closed his fingers around it, letting her hand linger on his for a moment. "I'm glad it helps."

"Yeah, it's good, Doc," Swifty closed his eyes and settled back. "I know you've got rounds, and I'm tired, so it won't be long before I'm asleep. But if anything happens to me, Doc, I need you to do me a favor."

Kit sat forward. "Of course, Slater. What is it?"

"Forgive yourself."

She reached out and tousled Slater's hair. "You're a kind man. Pull through this. Doctor's orders."

***

Kit sat in her office reviewing patient charts when she heard a commotion in the main hall. A deep voice, followed by a higher, female voice, and then another.

She stood up and huffed out a sigh, exiting the room.

"There. There she is, the murderer," Yina pointed at the doctor, and Kit held up her hands, taking a step forward. A look of open-mouthed confusion and surprise crossed her face, then a scowl of betrayal.

"You can call me what you like, Yina, but keep your voices down in here. This is a hospital, not Polly's Saloon." She grit her teeth into a wolfish snarl, then looked up at Diribe. "What's this about?"

"Thirty-seven people are dead because of you. You confessed to the murders yourself in Polly's Saloon less than two weeks ago, intentionally injecting them with stolen serum samples that you knew were tainted." Yina stuck her finger in Kit's face. "Polly and Yaja were with me when you confessed."

"Get your finger out of my face, Yina. If you're here to arrest me, then arrest me. Otherwise, I have work to do."

Kit looked at Diribe again, who gave her an apologetic look. "I don't believe the accusations, Doctor Judge, but

Yina's my deputy and the alleged confession is admissible as evidence under Southwest Territory law."

"I reserve and invoke my right to silence," Kit said.

"You have that right," he held up the chains and cuffs. "Come with me, then. We'll have to keep you in holding until the marshal comes." Diribe put the chains on Kit's wrists, and she let him. He took her gun belt and handed it to Yina. She let him do that, too. The deputy strapped on the belt as if it were her own.

"What about my patients?"

"They might survive without you poisoning them," Yina said, then spat at Kit's feet.

Kit looked down at the white foamy saliva, then back up at Yina. She said nothing, but her eyes burned as she glared at the woman. Yina stuck out her chin, defiant.

"You got something to say, Doctor?" She took a step forward.

Kit continued her stare. *I'm so close—too close.*

Yina looked away.

Diribe held out a hand between them. "Come with me now, Doctor. Yina, that's enough."

Yina gave him a look and then huffed her way out the door. Kit let Diribe lead her outside.

A crowd gathered near the hospital to see why Diribe and Yina had been so keen to head there, and they gaped at the Doctor being led in chains. They were silent, in shock, but Kit could hear their whispers as she walked to the jail.

What in the world? We need the doctor?! She was our chance—

Now what will we do?

Is she a murderer? Is she a thief?

What did she do?

This can't be real—

Diribe brought Kit inside and to the holding cell in the far back of the Sheriff's Office. He turned away as he took off her chains, then closed the cell door. "Yina, call for the Marshal. I'm going to talk to the doctor."

Yina smirked at Kit, then gave Diribe a grim nod. Once she was gone, Diribe turned back to the doctor, grabbed a chair, and sat down outside the cell.

"You're not going to act up," he said.

"You won't give me reason to act up," Kit looked him in the eyes. The gazes locked and she held it until he nodded.

"No, I won't. You care to make a statement?"

"No, I do not. I want an attorney, and I want details of these accusations. That's all." Kit gripped the jail's bars and stretched her mind, trying to scrape Diribe's. All she heard was static, like on the wireless at four in the morning. Sometimes the voices would fade in, and sometimes, just more static.

"Tell me about the caverns," Diribe said, spreading his hands.

Kit shrugged. "Tell me about the accusations, or let me read the warrant for my arrest."

"I'm not your enemy, Doctor," Diribe said. "I just want to get to the truth. See, Yina says you saw something in the caverns, some kind of people testing on other people, but when she went there, nothing but what you'd expect to find in normal caves—a lot of guano and water."

Kit stared straight ahead and down the long hall. From where she sat, she could see the front door and noted there were no blind spots at this angle. The entire cell seemed visible from the front desk, even though it was a good forty feet away.

"You are not my enemy, Sheriff, but you're not my friend, either. Attorney. Charges. Now."

Diribe sighed and shook his head. "Maybe Yina's right, and you've gone mad. I don't want to believe it, but you give me nothing, and I can't help you."

Kit scoffed, a snort of derision blowing through her lips. "Nice try, Sheriff."

The sheriff stood and dusted off the front of his pants, then walked to the front to talk to Yina. Kit put her hand over her eyes and tried to listen, but there was only the sound of static until her head ached and her nose dripped with blood.

Once she stopped the bleeding, Kit laid back and stared at the ceiling. She tried to rest. Couldn't.

Standing, the doctor paced back and forth, thinking about what changed. What made Yina decide to turn her in for murder? What changed her from a compassionate, potential friend to such a betrayal? She recalled a kiss on her forehead and kindness. Compassion. What happened to change that?

Kit rubbed the back of her neck as she paced and mulled it over, then pushing it aside to focus on her patients. She thought about trying to get a message to the nurse's aides, but it wasn't likely that the sheriff would cooperate. She wondered how Slater was faring.

Her ability to listen worked most of the time, but at the moment, either because of stress or by chance, she wasn't able to hear. *Nothing on the wireless tonight, Kathryn*, she heard Thomas Senior's voice in her head. *Let's go upstairs and see what else we can find.*

The scents of some sort of rotisserie game bird hit her nose and Kit sniffed the air. At least the nosebleed from earlier hadn't affected her sense of smell. Her stomach ached but there was no hunger there. Just a slow roll of nausea.

Diribe delivered her dinner. "Polly insisted you eat something. She says you're innocent, and Polly isn't one to be blinded by beauty and misled by smooth talkers." He opened the cell slot for her tray and slid it through. Kit took it.

"Is that so?" The doctor took an experimental bite of the game bird, and when she swallowed, her stomach began a tirade of hunger. She forced herself to eat slowly.

"That's so," Diribe said. "Rice, on the other hand, is calling for your blood."

"Rice, eh? Let him call," she said between mouthfuls. "Where's my attorney? You've got twelve more hours to secure me one."

"She'll be here to accompany you with the marshal. Not too many lawyers out here." Diribe scratched his evening scruff and leaned against the wall. "Hard part is, she comes with the marshal and you leave town with everyone thinking you're a murderer, if you even get out of town alive. See, out here, the marshal might decide on a hanging, lawyer or no."

Kit's eyes widened, and then she set her jaw. "Then let it be what it is, Sheriff. People can think as they please, and if I hang, I hang. Your threats are duly noted."

She resumed eating, though much slower the second time around, having lost any trace of her appetite.

After ignoring the sheriff for some time, the man stood straight again. "If you change your mind and want to make a statement, have Yina call on me. I'm going home. The marshal will be here either tomorrow night or by the day after tomorrow, in the morning. But this might be your last chance, Doctor Judge."

Kit looked down at her plate and took a drink of water from the cup. She looked back up and sighed. "Anything I say can be twisted to incriminate me. Therefore, I say nothing, Sheriff Onyemaechi."

"Would you write a statement if I left you a pen and paper?" Diribe fished around his pockets, but Kit shook her head.

"I don't see the point. Any words I write could be twisted, and you still haven't brought me the warrant." Kit took another drink and picked up the cigarette and match on her tray. They both seemed to disappear from her hand.

Diribe's eyebrows shot up and Kit could see more white in his eyes than brown. "Yina was supposed to bring them earlier. I'll make sure she does tonight."

"You can't detain me come morning if she doesn't," Kit resumed eating her roll. "Night, Sheriff."

Once Diribe realized she was going to continue ignoring him, the man left and she could hear him speaking to Yina in soft tones. She could hear the clack of typewriter keys and then Yina responding to him, but couldn't make out the words.

Plate clean, water cup empty, Kit set it aside and saved her cigarette and match.

***

She didn't sleep. No rest while her mind was turning, too busy dwelling on her situation, putting the pieces together. Rice was calling for her death. He was a traditionalist, so of course he wanted her dead. Traditionalists hated science, despised women and resented them being in power, and believed that there was some supernatural force that would eventually come from their fictional land and devour the world. Like the ones who tried to kill Mary Edwards Walker during the War of East and West, Rice believed that women who didn't fall in line with their ideas were to be raped and killed.

Their numbers had dwindled to near extinction since the 1500s, when the Alastor and Timeworn myths began to be questioned en masse. The cults began their battles for supremacy, and the scientists used this to advance reason and logic.

So was Yina a traditionalist, then? Set to take her down in any way possible? Was the offering of friendship a setup?

The dim, yellow lights in the sheriff's office were even dimmer towards the back, so much so that Kit was almost in the darkness. But she could see out just fine.

She closed her eyes and listened to the sounds of rustling paper, then footsteps coming closer. Kit opened one eye to see Yina holding the warrant in her hand.

"Bad news for you, Doctor."

"Since my son died, my life's been bad news." Kit struck her match against the wall and lit her cigarette, drawing in a deep breath. "Pass that warrant through."

"Not till you put out your match."

Kit barked a laugh. "If you really think I'd burn this with a single match, Yina, then you're as stupid as you are a liar." She blew out the match with a smoke-filled exhale, plumes of the gray haze wafting upward, then settling to form a lazy cloud. "Which is to say, you're incredibly stupid."

Yina scowled. "Take it."

She thrust the two pages through the cell's slot and they turned through the air, landing at Kit's feet. The doctor picked it up and read it.

"Says here I'm accused of premeditated murder," she tossed it aside. "It'll never stick."

"Doesn't have to stick. It just has to ruin you, or get Rice and his cult riled enough to rally up the sympathizers." Yina smiled. "And here you were, thinking you were surrounded by friends."

Kit took a deep drag from her cigarette and stood up, walking over just barely out of Yina's reach. She bent forward at the waist and blew the smoke in her face. "No. Not friends. But I thought you lot had potential."

Yina coughed and waved her hand. "I've got more bad news for you, Kathryn."

"Oh? What could be worse than my hanging?" Kit shrugged and stood back.

"Swifty's dead."

Yina's flat statement made Kit's legs buckle beneath her, and she reeled back to the bench to sit down. "No. He—you're lying."

"Dead from the poison you gave him. He said his heart was acting funny, and by the time Jessica got to him, he was gone." Yina's lips twitched. "So you can add Swifty to your body count."

"You're *happy* about this?" Kit looked up and snarled. "You're happy that Slater died while I was trying to help him. You're sick."

Yina scowled. "I'm not happy about Swifty's death. I'm happy that you're going to pay for your arrogance. You come into this town acting like you're some kind of savior, and expecting us to kiss your feet and treat you like a queen, when all you do is kill people. You murdered those people and now you're going to pay for it."

"I *didn't* murder them, Yina, but I am responsible. Like I told Diribe, if I hang, I hang." She polished off her cigarette and stamped it out with her boot. "Go away, Yina. Leave me to my thoughts."

"Sad about Swifty. He never knew the scorpion till it stung him."

Kit looked away and stared at the wall. Yina waited.

The doctor continued to ignore her, looking at the wall as she could feel Yina's eyes on the back of her head. After a moment, the deputy turned on her heel and left.

Hot tears ran down her cheeks mixed in with the sweat of the day and the doctor put her face in her hands so she wouldn't make a sound.

Curled up on the bench with her back to the wall, Kit fell into the gray of a thin sleep, images of Swifty and his 'aw, shucks' grin smiling at her. She reached out to touch his face, and his hand touched hers.

"You know what you saw," Swifty said. "You're not mad, and you know Yina is lying. You know the answers."

Kit woke with a start to the sound of metal against metal. She looked to her cell door.

"Polly insisted you get all her meals from her," Diribe said. "She'd come to visit, but we don't allow visitors for the first day."

"Thank her for the meals from me," Kit stood and rubbed her eyes, then took the tray. "I appreciate it."

"I will. You got anything to say about your accusations?" He pointed with his chin to the pages of the warrant on the floor. "Anything at all?"

Kit took her tray and sat down. “Just that it won’t stick, and I’ll wait for my lawyer to explain it to you. I’m sure you’re a bright man, Sheriff, so she won’t have to use small words.”

“Well I hope not,” Diribe said. “But who knows?”

“Guess we’ll have to find out,” Kit said. “When the marshal gets here.”

“Tonight or tomorrow.”

“Yep.”

Kit tucked into her breakfast and Diribe walked away.

HANGED UP

Rice could really gather a crowd. With help from his penitents, of course. They'd waited for what seemed like a hound's age for this moment. Seeing the arrogant, fat-lipped doctor in irons gave his heart a thrill he'd not felt since he first found this town and his penitents. He was going to sweep a path, now. Of course, that couldn't be done alone.

His group gathered around him, some dispersed through the gathering to help rally up the people. Rice worked them with his sermons. They didn't have to be believers, but all they had to do was listen.

Because Rice had a gift. He could *sway*.

Even when he was young, he could get crowds to change their minds about virtually anything, but it had to be when they were at their most vulnerable. Catch them confused or in crisis, and *swaying* was easy. It was how he got so many penitents from this town alone.

Using the right pitch and tone, he rocked the crowd to the *sway* and more people started to gather and listen. That gave him an even better platform to take care of this troublemaker, and maybe even give himself a foothold over this town. It'd been a long time for him and for his penitents. They were only fifty in number, but they might be able to get those numbers up even more with what was happening now.

At first the people had turned to the doctor for answers, but now, with people continuing to die and the loss of sweet Gemini (beloved by so many, and so often), it gave them doubts. Doubts in science. Doubts in what worked, what healed.

It was his chance to come in and save them all. *Sway them all.* He smirked.

"Now you tell me, with this 'doctor' up on murder charges, and this poison of hers killing people in our town, to whom should we turn? Who should we trust?" Rice smiled from atop his perch, his soapbox. "No, I don't ask you to turn to Alastor today, nor tomorrow. What I ask of you is, where will you put your faith now that science has failed you?"

"Tell us, Parson Rice," one of his penitents called out from the back. There were murmurs of assent from around her.

He waved one hand in a grand motion. “This land is blessed; an oasis in the desert. Now while I’m sure doctors are fine for helping you through the occasional illness, there are some who are stinging scorpions. This one—and I’m sure you will agree—this one is one of the stingers.”

A few calls of assent, some of disbelief. Rice had to work harder the larger the crowd got.

“Oh, like some of you, I wouldn’t have believed it myself until Deputy Ndubuisi showed me the charges. Thirty-seven counts of murder, and now, thirty-eight for poor dear Gemini Hsiao.” He took his hat off and held it to his chest. “My friends and fellow townsfolk—can we allow that to pass? Can we allow this so-called doctor, or butcher, to escape justice?”

A wagon grew bigger in the distance, headed straight for the Platt’s Gulch entrance.

The crowd swelled with louder cries for justice, and Rice pushed his *sway* to its limits. “I say to you, that we turn to our Right of Vengeance upon this murderer and take her life for all the lives she’s taken.”

His head was starting to throb and his heart hammered hard enough that he thought it might burst, but he kept it up as he saw two people—a man and a woman—exit the marshal's wagon. The woman wore an expensive suit and her braids were slicked back on her head. She carried a briefcase and a hateful expression at the crowd. The marshal was a tall man, as tall as Diribe, and carried ropes on him.

"You're here for the doctor," Rice said as the crowd parted to let the two of them through. He looked at the woman. "*You* must be her attorney." He said it as if he were holding back vomit.

"We're here for Doctor Judge," the marshal said, and the attorney stood back, still sour-faced, looking at the crowd.

"She's here, in the jailhouse, Marshal," Rice stepped to the edge of his pulpit but not off it, preferring the height advantage. "But we're calling for a hanging today."

"My client gets a fair trial," the attorney said. The marshal held up his hand at her and she scowled.

"You're new around here, Pilar," the marshal looked down at her and flicked his chains over one arm, like a waiter carrying a serviette for patrons. "But in this territory, the town has the final say."

Rice and the marshal exchanged looks and the marshal tipped his hat.

"You the mayor? I'm Marshal Albert Deringer. This here is Pilar Nguyen, and she's not too happy about the lay of the land as you can see." The marshal shrugged. "She'll get over it."

Pilar brushed by them and entered the jailhouse, letting the door slam behind her.

"Or maybe she won't," Deringer said. "Woman had a fire ant picnic in her pants on the way here—that's of no consequence, though. So, as I asked, you the mayor?"

Rice greeted him with his hand to his heart and raised his fist. "No sir, Marshal. I'm the town's Parson. No mayor. The Sheriff runs the town just fine."

"So what did the town decide?" The marshal took a look around at the crowd who seemed wound up enough that he knew what they decided.

Rice smiled, seeming proud of himself. "They decided on a hanging, here, and now. Right of Vengeance."

Deringer shrugged. "Who am I to argue with the public?"

***

Diribe and Pilar stood inside and spoke in tones Kit couldn't hear. She couldn't listen—too much interference with the crowd. If she tried to strain, that many voices and that much anger might make her nose bleed without stopping. Instead, she tried to read their lips.

"They're out there calling for a lynching," Pilar said, raising her hands to either side of her head. She splayed her fingers and held her hands stiff. "It's insane."

Diribe nodded. "It is, but your client stands accused of thirty-eight counts of murder and the people want swift justice. They don't care to hear her side."

"Accused, not convicted."

"People are idiots, but the law out here is—"

"Yes, yes—so you say the law out here is different. So says Marshal Deringer. This mob justice is murder, and if you let it happen, I'll have you put on trial." Pilar folded her arms across her chest and looked up at the sheriff.

"You can, of course, and I'd stop them if I could but when they get like this, they'd lynch the three of us if we tried to stop them. It doesn't happen often, but what can I do?" Diribe looked back at the cell and then at Pilar. "What can I do—I mean that."

"It's not that difficult, Sheriff. You have a gun. A shotgun, even." Pilar turned away and looked out the window at the crowd. "Maybe there isn't anything to be done."

Kit stopped reading their lips and turned away, heart beating a slow, hard rhythm. "I'm going to die for these assholes," she ran a hand through her hair and stopped to rub her neck. "Unbelievable."

The clock over Diribe's head inched towards noon, and Kit paced the floor while Pilar made her way back to the cell. "I'm going to send a message to the Western Guard and get them to assist with enforcing the law," Pilar put her hand on her chest and raised it in greeting. "I'm Pilar Nguyen, by the way."

Kit returned the gesture. "Kathryn Judge. You can try to get the Guard here, but I think they won't make it in time." She shrugged. "Thanks for trying, though."

The doctor turned away and Pilar walked out towards the front office again, telling Diribe she was contacting the Western Guard.

Diribe stepped back, then turned at the door's noise. A dry squeak at the hinges, footsteps.

The marshal introduced himself and handed over the paperwork to pull Kit from her cell. When Kit turned, she could only stand at the bars and watch each of them with the cool-eyed measure of sizing them up.

The biggest insult was that Yina still had possession of her gun. Her fingers itched at the thought of that loss. She leaned forward with her forehead resting on one of the crossbars, watching the exchange of paperwork.

Diribe spent as much time as he could reading the orders, turning the pages and glancing back over his shoulder at Pilar, who was speaking to someone in her native tongue. He stared at her a moment, not able to decipher the sounds from individual words, but it ate up time to figure it out. Diribe went back to reading.

Then he could dawdle no longer. Diribe grimaced and signed his part of the paperwork, hand feeling as though it'd been stung by a hundred bees. He handed the papers back to the marshal, then gave him a raised eyebrow and tipped his chin upward. "You new to the area? I don't recall ever meeting you out here in the Gulch."

"Just got assigned to this sector, actually. I'd been working in Heckler's Gorge till last month."

Diribe shrugged. “I have a cousin who works in Heckler’s Gorge. You know Nwankwo Madukaego?”

“Can’t say that I do,” the marshal said, “unless he goes by another name.”

“You should know him if you worked in Heckler’s Gorge,” Diribe said, scowling. He reached for the butt of his gun. “He would’ve been your boss.”

The marshal reached out with one hand and put it over Diribe’s throat. With a wet, sucking sound, the man with the graying walrus mustache ripped out the windpipe in one fluid movement. Diribe’s eyes went wide, but there was no sound other than a rushing of air. The meat in the marshal’s palm slid to the ground.

His other hand grabbed his six shooter and shot Pilar in the head. The bullet made a small hole in the front of her skull, and the back blew out as if it popped off in two.

“All that jabbering just to make a simple phone call to the Guard. You shouldn’t have stopped to handle your sister’s baby problems,” Deringer chuckled, then sniffed the muzzle of his revolver. “Now they’ll never know.” He holstered his six-shooter and turned back to the cell, taking his time with each step.

At first, Kit couldn't make sense of what happened. She stood in her cell, hands gripping the bars so tight her knuckles ran white. Her heart pounded in her ears as she looked at the mess from the other room. Diribe stopped twitching once he lost enough blood, and the back of Pilar's head made a rust-colored sunburst all over the side wall.

Deringer didn't have to bend too far to look right into Kit's eyes.

"Time to hang, interloper."

THE SWIFT EXCHANGE

Cords. Cords hanging from the scaffolding, thick and pliable, one wrapped in an elegant noose. Cords stretching in sharp relief from the doctor's neck as she thrashed against the marshal, crowd hollering and whooping for blood. The influx of whispers told Kit that it wasn't her they wanted, it was bloodlust. They were like the buzzing of bees—drones in swarms just milling about from flower to flower, and for now, her flower was the most succulent.

She still kicked and thrashed against the marshal who held her with his too-strong hands. He tied her own behind her back and dragged her to the hanging platform.

Rice's penitents were the ones really enjoying it, and the doctor realized those were the ones whooping and cheering—they were the ones calling for her blood. She marked their faces by their whispers. The penitents were a mix of men and women, and even as Kit struggled against the marshal, she committed their faces to memory. The rest of the crowd stood, stunned, bemused, watching in rapture just to see what would happen next.

No one rips a man's throat out quite like that with common strength, Kit thought—*and now he's got me good.*

The doctor's hands stole away at the ties that clasped her wrists together, picking the knots out as fast as she could while still thrashing. She needed Deringer to be distracted by her kicks and tripping him while they walked. It would keep him from catching on to what she was doing.

Picking up their pace, the marshal dragged her to the stairs, giving Kit an advantage. She dropped low and put one foot on the bottom step, then one on the top, and pushed backwards. It was enough to take Deringer off balance and bring them both back to the bottom of the steps.

In order to stay on his feet, the marshal had to lean forward and look down at the ground. Kit did a pratfall and rolled to face the crowd, angled away from them and from Deringer.

That gave her enough time to undo two of the knots.

Deringer let out a rumble that was more of a strangled cry, then grabbed the doctor by her hair and pulled her into a standing position. Kit felt her scalp tear and gritted her teeth, letting out a low growl. She stood, feeling pools trickle down her temples with more speed than the sweat that was pouring off her. Some dripped onto her lips and she licked them, tasting the iron and copper traces. Blood.

He'd pulled her hair hard enough to rip into her scalp. Judging by how he'd killed Diribe, though, she wasn't all that surprised. Her head was on fire, but she wasn't shocked by what he could do.

The pain in her scalp was plenty, and the crowd's whispers piled on, making her head throb and her nose start a thin drip. Deringer laughed at her. "Guess I pulled a bit too hard, didn't I?"

Kit sneered at him and sniffled up some of the blood. A coppery tang in the back of her throat came back to her, and she swallowed.

Facing the crowd, the doctor looked above their heads, past them and to the hospital. Her guts burned and she stared at the doors. All she'd wanted to do was help them, and this was her payment.

You're no murderer.

That voice…

Kit knew that whisper—familiar as her own son's voice. From that whisper came a shout and the doors to the hospital opened with what sounded like a bullet from a gun. "No! You can't hang the doctor. She's cured us."

Heads turned and Kit could hear the whispers change from hostile and lusting to stunned and curious. While the cultists were still eager to see her hang, the entire sick ward had emerged and met their loved ones. Cries of joy and laughter bubbled up toward the scaffold and Kit could see people hugging as they were reunited with the cured.

The ropes on the doctor's wrists came undone, and she started to reach up to take the noose off her neck, but the floor dropped out from underneath her. Marshal Deringer grinned, hand still on the lever. He laughed.

Pain seared through Kit's neck as she gagged and gasped for air. Her hands came up to her neck and the noose tightened. She didn't kick—instead holding her legs stiff and still as she tried to get her fingers in between her neck and the rope.

Swifty saw Yina standing proud, watching Kit swing, and saw she was wearing the doctor's gun belt. He reached out and yanked it off her, then aimed above Kit's head.

Yina reached over and made a grab for it, sending the first bullet flying into the air, hitting the town's emergency bell. It made a clang and resounding ring. Swifty elbowed Yina in the face as hard as he could. She reeled back, and Swifty fired again.

This time, it hit, going through the rope. Kit fell through the scaffolding and gripped the structure, easing her fall to the ground. She choked and sputtered, retching as she took in great gulps of air. Her vision ceased to double as she breathed, and she recovered herself as Swifty exchanged fists with Yina.

Beloved Swifty—a good person to many in Platt's Gulch—had his share of support. Others grabbed at Yina and tried to hold her back from the young man. She struggled against them but there were enough working against her to keep the woman from breaking free.

Kit hobbled over towards Swifty to retrieve her gun, but stopped and turned when the marshal let out a roar of anger at the crowd. She looked up at the nearby scaffold to see him come after her, jumping off the death stage with the grace of a pouncing wildcat. Kit side-stepped to avoid his landing on top of her, not eager to have her body torn to shreds the way he'd ripped apart Diribe.

The marshal drew his gun and aimed it at her. She ran for a nearby concrete wall and ducked behind it, peeking out to see Deringer fire into the crowd.

There was no way the doctor would allow him to punish the crowd when she was the one he wanted. *Let me be damned, then.* Kit ran out toward the marshal, and time seemed to come to a stop. She turned to see Swifty with her gun, and he tossed it to her.

Aim for his eyes, the voice whispered. It was Swifty's voice, clear and strong in her head. No tickle or burn of an impending nosebleed. She caught the gun and took aim, moving fast enough that the marshal didn't have time to do more than look in her direction.

She fired twice, barely moving the muzzle for each eye.

Thick crimson fluid that looked more dense than human blood poured out of the marshal, and his body shifted and twisted into something that wasn't human. It had a silvery, scaly body and its head was shaped more like a drawn heart, with a frowning slit for a mouth, holes for nostrils, no discernable nose, and large eye sockets.

Amid the chaos, the townspeople shrieked and gasped, looking at the thing that was twitching on the ground and watching it die from the loss of its blood.

Yina pulled away from the people who were holding her—they were too stunned to keep gripping her tight enough—and drew in a breath. When she let it out, it came with a high-pitched shriek that made the crowd cover their ears. Kit tried to take aim, but the sound from Yina was too loud, and she covered her ears as well.

When she stopped, the ground began to rumble, but not from an earthquake. Kit looked to the horizon and gasped.

Near the foothills, the horizon was awash with silvery-scaled creatures. They had no weapons, only their strength and speed.

"Children, take cover," Kit raised her voice to be heard over the panic, and she turned to the adults as the children in the crowd scattered to hide. "If you have weapons, prepare to fight. Aim for their eyes."

She could hear the clack-clack of single-action revolvers being prepared as well as people running indoors if they were unarmed. Some emerged once more with weapons in hand, ready to fight. Others hid, helping the children stay safe.

Yina leapt at Kit, launching herself forward to grab at the woman's hair, but Kit was ready. She fired again, aiming for her eyes.

Kit's aim had been excellent in the weeks that she walked, hunting for her food and bagging small game. Even with the ground shaking and the hordes of scaled-beings running over the land to engage in battle, her aim was true.

She hit Yina's left eye and blood—that scarlet oil—poured out of it. She fired again to hit the other eye.

A scaled creature knocked her off balance and her arm flailed to the side, hitting the stomach of another scaled creature that was devouring the entrails of a townie Kit didn't recognize. The creature took in the bullet as if she'd put a pin in a pin cushion. It took no notice and kept ripping the townie apart.

Kit turned to face the creature that had knocked her off balance and it wrested the revolver from her hand. She made a grab for it, but the creature slapped her hands away and leaned forward. Its jaws snapped at her neck and Kit pulled back in time to keep herself from being bitten. She made a second attempt to grab her revolver.

It raised the gun and fired.

The heat was the first thing she felt as the bullet penetrated her stomach. When she was younger, her grandfather showed her the art of making bullets for his antique musket. The perfect sphere from the mold always came out a bright red-orange glow, and Kit would put her cold hands near it to feel the heat. She wasn't stupid enough to actually touch it, but that heat nearly blistered her palms just the same. It felt as though that heat was inside her body, radiating through her torso.

Doctor Judge didn't have the stamina that the scaled creature had—there was no taking this bullet and moving forward. She put her hands over the wound and looked down at the dark blood—the black blood—oozing out of her and onto her pale palms. Bile. Liver. She'd been hit in the liver.

Searing heat spread up her neck as she fell forward, and she heard the creature make a laughing sound. Her vision blurred, and she fought to hang on, pressing her hands harder into her guts. She felt a giddiness wash over her as she went into shock, and the pain seemed to be distant. Kit laughed as a tunnel formed in front of her, winnowing down to a pinpoint of light.

The Walking Doctor laughed all the way into the darkness.

WALKING HOME

Boots on the hardpan, spurs jingling with each step, the Walking Doctor looked down at her feet, then up at the sky. Cirrus clouds, wispy and thin, made promises of rain against the azure backdrop. She sighed and halted her walk, looking around the landscape.

Dotted with Joshua trees and saguaro cacti in the distance, there was nothing around her but more hardpan. She frowned, picking a direction.

A sidewinder made its way past her, and she froze in place, observing it. The creature didn't rattle, and continued its business past as it headed for the hilly lands behind her.

Scales. Hills.

That created the feeling of tiny bubbles popping inside of her stomach—a giddy feeling that told her something was familiar, but she couldn't understand what. The doctor looked at the sidewinder as it made faint patterns against the hardpan. The sunlight gave its scales a mirror quality. She'd never seen a skin quite like it. It was coppery, blending in with the clay color of the hills, but shiny. It was hypnotic watching the snake move. The doctor took a deep breath as more tickles engaged her stomach. A feeling of déjà vu took over her mind, and she felt swimmy for a minute. She closed her eyes and opened them again.

Where in Perdition was she?

Kit watched the sidewinder get smaller and disappear into the distance, then turned back to the direction she'd been facing.

What was happening?

Looking down at herself, she saw a hole in her shirt, and touched its edges with her finger. A bullet hole the size of her pinkie. She'd been shot?

Where was the blood?

With a huff, Kit looked off to her left and saw a large tree, or what was left of the thing. It looked petrified, forever in a bent position as if blown back by some memory of wind. She started toward it, then hesitated.

What if it was the wrong way?

The Walking Doctor felt for her pouch on her shoulder, but the pouch wasn't there. That meant her compass was missing, and that meant she was lost.

Fine.

She espied a figure underneath the tree, emerged from behind it. The figure was that of a man, shorter than she, and busy, paying his surroundings no mind. Kit watched him as he laid down bits of wood and made a small pile. The doctor stayed back and still, sniffing the gentle breeze and the dry air that carried a sweet scent of desert flowers on it.

The man sparked something, and a fire grew in the wood pile. Kit started to walk again. Toward him. She felt for her gun, but the holster was empty.

That was enough to make her stop. She wasn't so sure about approaching a stranger without her sidearm.

Do it. Trust that instinct. It won't fail you.

Her mother's voice whispered that to her, words that she always told her when Kit had reached an impasse. She heeded it and started walking again, letting the feeling of vulnerability lie.

The figure grew and Kit thought she recognized him, but couldn't place him. He had dark blonde hair and a crooked smile, and he removed his hat when she approached.

"Been waiting for you to come around. Sit, please," he said, and she did.

"Where am I?" Kit looked up at the man with the slight scruff and the gentle eyes.

"You know where you are—the desert."

"No I get that, but I just—I was fighting. I was in some sort of fight and I got shot." Kit showed him her shirt and the man reached out to touch the bullet hole.

"How about that? But you're not bleeding, are you?" The man hunkered down so they were eye-level.

Kit shook her head. "No, and I'm confused."

"You hit your head on the way down. But don't worry. I know just what you have to do, Kathryn Judge."

Hearing her name felt like a splash of ice water to her face. She backed away and put her hand over her heart. "I'm Kathryn Judge. I'm a doctor. I walked to Platt's Gulch and there was an attack. Now I'm here, in the desert, and you're Swift Slater. Right?" She rubbed the back of her neck and then brought her hands to her face. "I'm here, in the desert. With you."

Swifty smiled at her and bent onto both his knees. "That's right. And do you know what you have to do?"

Kit shook her head.

"Wake up."

***

The doctor's eyes opened to the snaps and pops of a campfire, and she lay on some kind of a bedroll. Overhead, the fat stars and milky swirls in the sky looked down at her, seeming closer without the light of the moon.

"Oh, you're awake. I was wondering when that might happen." Swifty greeted her with a smile and put a bowl to her lips. "Here, my friend. Drink this. It'll help your strength."

Kit sat up on her elbows and felt one of Swifty's hands press into her back to keep her propped up. The other hand held the bowl steady and he tipped it as she drank.

A sweet, thick and milky liquid ran down her throat. It reminded the doctor of condensed milk but with a hint of coffee to it. She drank until the bowl was empty.

"Perfect. You'll feel a might better soon," Swifty rubbed her back a moment, then let her decide if she wanted to lie back down or not.

The doctor sat upright and stared at him. "Slater? You seem—well—you seem different."

Swifty smiled. "How so, Doc?"

"Your demeanor. I mean, you're usually sweet, it's true, but you seem more confident. Sure of yourself." Kit cocked her head. "What in Perdition happened?"

"You got shot back there, in Platt's Gulch. When the people around you saw that happen, the chaos seemed to come to a head, and the people started to fight back harder than ever. For justice. They fought for their lives because you fought for them." Swifty spread out his hands and set the bowl down by the fire. "Your death pretty much saved our town."

Kit shook her head. "No, no it didn't. You lot did that."

Swifty grinned. "Agreed, Doc. Agreed."

"I'm not dead—I can still feel things," Kit frowned, then looked at Swifty again. "Right?"

"That's right, Doc, you're not dead. Not anymore." He laughed and poured another bowl of liquid. "Here, drink some more. You need it."

"What is it?" Kit sniffed the contents. It smelled like a confection of coffee and white chocolate. She drank.

"It's a concoction I made from a recipe my great-grandmother taught me. It's from a medicinal plant called 'mozhuatil.' Mozhuatil is one of the medicines the M'aqual discovered about three hundred years ago and they used to make it to cure just about everything. Funny thing is, I didn't remember it until today. Most people—including the M'aqual, don't even remember it." He shrugged. "It doesn't really cure everything, but it enhances your body's healing abilities, but it's hard to come by."

"So it's one of those that got pushed to the wayside except by some of the M'aqual," Kit said, taking another sip.

"Yeah—it'd actually been long lost until I recalled Nona Sopawi telling me about it." Swifty grinned. "But it all came back to me, and in good time, too."

Kit looked up at the man with bright interest as she drank. "Tell me, then. Teach me about it, Slater. Where'd you find it? What's the dosage?"

Swifty shrugged. "I'll write it all down for you so it won't be forgotten. It's a complex chemical chain, and the chemical compounds are binary. You have to put it with another plant, Ceratonia siliqua, to activate it."

"I didn't know that Ceratonia siliqua grew here in the Union, especially in the desert. I thought locust beans were imported." Kit took another drink. "How does it taste like chocolate?"

Swifty grinned. "That's the mozhuatil. It has a chocolate-like flavor that gets enhanced by the locust bean."

"So is it a stimulant?" Kit drank a little more of it. "It's certainly making me feel more awake and alive."

Swifty shook his head and took out a piece of paper and pencil, then began to draw. "No, it's not a stimulant. Sometimes it has sedative effects." He scribbled something down, then presented it to Kathryn.

She reached out for the paper and scanned it, then examined it more intently. A chemical formula. "Mozhuatil and Ceratonia siliqua come together to create this compound. Your great-grandmother told you this?"

Swifty shook his head. "Nona Sopawi was no chemist, but she was a healer. She knew her plant lore and kept it a secret. It was better for trade if what she did seemed like magic."

Kathryn sat back, silent. "Does it enhance everything, really?" Another sip, and she finished the second bowl.

"This enhances your phagocytes and lymphocytes without the risk of having them attack healthy tissue, and you'll have stronger antibodies later. I might start researching it with vaccines, see if we can improve them for the fight against polio." Swifty scratched his scruff, then leaned forward and stoked the fire.

"And you just remembered all of this abruptly, *and* recalled how and why it works?" Kit's eyebrows knitted together and her lips pursed into a frown. "You were obviously bright from the first time I met you, but you seemed unsure of your intelligence and not so confident when it came to pathology and chemistry. Now, you seem more—"

"Knowledgeable?" Swifty grinned. "Intelligent?"

"Assured, I was going to say, but yes, you seemed to be enhanced in a way." Kit sniffed the night air and gazed up at the stars, then back down to Swifty. "Yes, enhanced. That's what I'd call you for certain."

"It's okay, you're not all the way healed yet, but yes, I'm a better version of myself for my illness."

"Explain."

"Well, you know that serum you used?" He pointed to the vial around her neck. "The one you mixed with the serum I swiped from the laboratory?"

"Yes." Kit put her hand to the vial, and then clasped the picture of her son in her hand.

"Well, it worked. It didn't just wipe out the cause of my illness, it rewired me, in a way. Enhanced some of my genetics, unlocked some memories, and encoded me with additional information." Swifty gave her a smile and stood up. "Excuse me a moment. Our supper is cooking in the ground."

Kit watched the young man get up and disappear behind the campfire. She heard him dig, and soon, the smells of roasted quail hit her nose. She took a deep inhale.

The sounds of tin plates and liquid pouring echoed in the air, and a coyote howled in the distance, answered by another in the opposite direction. Kit brought her knees to her chest and smiled to herself. She didn't ache like she expected. Her wound seemed distant, muscles sore, but manageable.

When she saw Swifty again, holding two plates, she unbent herself and took one. Her stomach growled.

"I can't believe how hungry I am. How long have we been out here?" Kit tucked into her game bird and took her coffee from Swifty's outstretched hand, muttering her thanks as she did.

"Oh, about a week. It took some time to heal your wounds, but the formula worked. I stopped the bleeding. Your liver had a bullet in it, but that came out on day three." Swifty settled down next to her, but angled his body so they could look at each other when they spoke.

"I spent a week unconscious?" Kit shook her head, then resumed eating. "Out here?"

Swifty laughed. "Yeah, out here. I dragged you off the battlefield and put you in a wagon, then carted you out here. I just—I knew what to do."

"Clearly." Kit sipped her coffee and let everything he said process. She sighed. "So you stopped the bleeding with what?"

"Apo-kapa. It's a cactus that clots blood. I used the juice in the wound via a small tube, then waited. It looked bad for the first day. You stopped bleeding in a hurry, but I thought you lost too much blood. But it went from black to red, to nothing. After that, you were in and out of consciousness."

Kit shook her head and chewed a mouthful of game bird. She swallowed and shrugged her shoulders. "I don't remember any of it. I wasn't conscious, just automatic."

Swifty pulled apart some of his bird and let it cool in the night air. "That's more of what it was. Just following my commands. But I'm glad you trusted me to do it. Somewhere deep inside there, you trusted me."

The doctor looked at Swifty and gave him a soft smile. "I do trust you, consciously and otherwise."

They ate in silence for awhile, listening to the sounds of the desert. Coyotes howling and yipping, crickets trumpeting, owls hooting to brag about their catches, and the crackles from the fire became their music.

Kit was the one to break the silence. "How did you just know what to do? I mean, was it from the enhancements?"

Swifty nodded. "Yes, ma'am. I didn't just receive Nona's memories, you know. I received—well, it's a bit difficult to believe, but—" The man shrugged and frowned.

"Considering everything that's happened, Swifty, with scaly snake people who have superhuman strength and laboratory facilities hidden in a mountain range, I doubt that anything you say to me will be beyond my belief. I can stretch." Kit chuckled and Swifty grinned.

"I suppose that's so," he said as he cleaned his plate, throwing the bones in the fire. They made little popping noises as they disappeared into the bright yellow and orange flames. "Well, as it turns out, those alien creatures, whatever they are, aren't from Terra. They're from a place fairly far from here." He pointed up at a cluster of six stars. "From there, actually. In the Felis Catus constellation."

Kit stopped eating and followed Swifty's hand, gazing up at the two stars that symbolized the cat's ears, then down at its four 'feet,' and finally to its tail. She looked back at him, then finished her plate, tossing the bones into the fire. "Go on, Slater. I believe you."

Swifty put his bedroll behind him and leaned back on it. "Well, those creatures—those people, I suppose—they're conquerors. They came from a world where their climate is a lot like our desert. At least their Eastern hemisphere. The Western hemisphere was much colder and wetter. They were overpopulated and looking to move to the other hemisphere, but the other people in the Western hemisphere gave them an inhospitable climate. So they changed it."

Kit's jaw dropped. "They *changed* it? How?"

"I'm missing some of those details, sadly. They did something with carbon dioxide, warming the planet. They managed to exterminate the Westerners almost into oblivion." Swifty pointed to his arm. "All that's left of them is in here."

Swifty paused and looked over at Kit who was now turned to face him, giving him her undivided attention. "They were a fairly advanced people living in relative isolation, and by the time they realized they were under attack, they didn't have time to develop weapons and fight back. Not in the sense that you and I think of fighting."

Kit nodded for him to continue.

"They fought back by encoding DNA with messages. Actual messages that, when interacting with another's DNA—particularly a primate's—would give them memories and messages of who they were, and what to do if the snake people tried to conquer another place."

The doctor scowled. "Wait. How did they wind up here, then? It's not like the snake people would willingly carry something potentially dangerous to them."

Swifty shrugged. "An ally, double-agent, or something else, I guess. They didn't include that in their encoding."

Kit drank her coffee and set down the tin on top of her empty plate with a light clatter. "What did they look like, I wonder?"

"They didn't add that, either. I suppose appearances didn't matter to them." Swifty chuckled. "I like to imagine they looked like bears."

The doctor laughed. "I'd like that. The bear people."

Falling silent again, Kit settled down on her bedroll, and inched closer to the fire. "Tell me more, Slater, but stop if I fall asleep. I think that sedative effect hit me pretty hard."

Swifty grinned and moved his bedroll so that he was head-to-head with the woman. "Sure thing, Doc. There are important things to tell you, but there's time. There's time."

Kit closed her eyes and listened to the rise and fall of Swifty's voice about other things, and when the words drifted into lullabies, she saw the bear people in lab coats, working at a feverish pace to save what little was left of their kind.

***

"You shot three rattlers," Swifty said as he turned some hash over in the skillet over the morning fire.

Kit had returned from her morning facilities and gave him a look of disbelief. "I didn't."

"You did. Woke me up just before dawn. Three quick shots, and then you fell back on your bedroll without saying a word." Swifty's eyebrows shot up in surprise. "You don't remember?"

The doctor looked down at her gun belt, then her bedroll, giving a deep scowl. After a moment, a look of pleased recollection came over her face. "I do," she started to laugh. "I heard them rattling. It woke me and I thought they were coming after me—no idea what they were on about but I wasn't having any of it. I just reacted and then went back to sleep. Sorry I woke you."

Swifty laughed along with her. "Don't worry about it, Doc. I spent the morning cleaning them and working them into a nice hash with potatoes."

Kit sat down and poured out coffee for both of them. "Rattlesnake hash. Sounds intriguing."

"By the way, you lost something a little while ago. I've been meaning to see you get it back."

She cocked her head. "Oh?"

Her curiosity was sated when Slater pulled her familiar, weathered hat from his rucksack and handed it to her. "You can't be out here without your hat, Doc."

She grinned wide and put the hat on her head. "Thank you, Slater. I can't tell you how much I appreciate it."

"Doc, it's your own hat."

"Yes, I know, but you had it with you this whole time—you kept it safe."

He chuckled. "I do my best."

They ate breakfast and Kit stretched out, finding her rucksack and extracting her doctor's kit. She listened to her internal organs and nodded. "I'm recovered, almost completely now."

"You seem much stronger," Swifty said, cleaning off the plates and putting them away in their box. He got up and put the box in the wagon, which sat on the other side of a line of brambles.

“I feel it.” Kit took a deep breath. “A bit tired, but nothing that I can’t heal with a bit of exercise.”

“Sounds like there’s a ‘but’ in there,” Swifty said when he returned. He sat down on his bedroll. “Am I right?”

“Of course you are,” she grinned at him. “But first I want to hear more about the race of people who were killed.”

“The ones we called the bear people last night?” Swifty cracked his knuckles and sat forward.

“Yes, them. Tell me as much as you’re willing to share. We should find shade in the wagon, though. The sun’s going to be a monster today, I think.”

NEWFOUND ALLIES

The doctor and nurse settled into the covered wagon. During the heat of the day, the animals quieted, and the only sounds around them were their voices and the wind that picked up now and then. The shade made for a comfortable place to talk.

"Well, the people who developed this encoding didn't know it would even work in other species, but they were stuck. They had to do something rather than let themselves die." Swifty put up his hands in a 'who knows' gesture.

"Anyone would in their situation," Kit said. "If we had the means and technology, certainly we'd do the same thing if we were caught without weaponry that could defeat our enemy."

"Certainly, Doc." Swifty kept himself busy with a lap bench, cutting up locust beans and mozhuatil, then setting them in a jar filled with water. "And either the invaders knew what they had and kept it for security reasons, or they just didn't know what they had."

Kit cleaned her revolver as she listened, but said nothing. She nodded to indicate she was listening.

"The only reason this serum worked in humans, Doc, is because of what lies around your neck. What's left of it." Swifty pointed to her necklace again.

"My serum. The sample I made?" She shook her head. "How?"

"You told Polly and Yaja that you thought the serum you sampled from was tainted. It wasn't. When you created your copy, you created a new complex entirely. That's no longer Esther's Compound in that vial. That's Judge's Compound. You tried to improve on it, didn't you?" Swifty stared into her eyes and Kit swallowed, feeling her face heat, but not from the warm breeze.

"I did. But how do you know all this? You were sick when I was—" Kathryn gasped and put her hand over her mouth. "You're—"

Swifty stopped her with an upheld hand, then pointed to his temple. "I'm a listener, too."

The doctor frowned and uncovered her mouth, putting her cleaned revolver back together and reloading one by one instead of her usual moon clips. She holstered the gun, giving what he said some thought. "Have you always been that way?"

He nodded. “As long as I can remember, but never this well. When I was enhanced, I could listen to the whispers without consequences. Headaches, nosebleeds, tooth pain—” he snapped his fingers. “Gone. Now I just hear the whispers when they come.”

Kathryn sighed. “Maybe I should inject myself with the serum, then.” She ran her hand through her hair, and her face brightened. “Hey, remember back in the cave, when I doubled over from the sound in my head and sprung a nosebleed?”

Swifty nodded. “Scared me—I didn’t realize what was happening.”

“I gathered,” Kit said. “But why weren’t you overwhelmed with the noise?”

The nurse shrugged. “Not sure why. I think you were targeted.”

Targeted. Kit didn’t respond right away. After a moment, she sat forward.

“Alright, then, so tell me what my serum has to do with it. ‘The Judge’s Compound,” the doctor snorted a derisive laugh, then rolled her shoulders.

"The compound you created wasn't complete. It needed its binary companion—the encoded serum that was created by the bear people." Swifty stopped cutting up the plants and put the rest of them in the jar, removing the seal from a bottle of apple cider vinegar. He poured that into the mixture and watched as the brown liquid began to develop streaks of white. Once it did, he capped the jar and brought out a wax stick, melting it with the matches he had.

He put a thick seal around the jar and set it aside as Kit sat back and watched him. "When those two compounds came together," he said, "it created exactly what was needed to combat what the snake people were doing to the humans."

Kit bit her lower lip. "Experimenting on them."

"Experimenting."

"I can only assume it's to conquer us, then?" Kit shifted where she was sitting, whole body itching to get up and run outside into the desert.

"They likely do. It's either a way to conquer by killing or by mutating us, but it wasn't working. Hence the deaths." Swifty raised his hands. "I can listen without consequence now, but it didn't improve the skills, exactly."

Kit gave a wry chuckle. "You can't have it all, Slater."

"That's the truth," he laughed and sat back, then turned serious again.

The doctor shook her head. "I'm glad I was wrong."

"About what, Doc?" Swifty cocked his head at her.

"When we were attacked—I was expecting advanced weaponry. But they only had guns, and their strength in hand-to-hand combat."

Swifty nodded. "Surprised me, too. I guess they use bioweapons—conquering others with, well, whatever they've developed against us."

"Right."

They were silent again, listening to the breeze pick up, dust hitting the sides of the wagon.

"The bear people—this was their final act of vengeance on the snake people," Swifty said. "They weren't without recourse, in a way."

"I feel like you're holding back from me, Swift." The doctor sat up straight and pointed to her midsection. "Don't bother. I'm healing and I'm strong. Anything you tell me, I can take."

THE PROPHECY

"Along the way, my children, Ursala the Prophetess died, but passed the stories onto her children. That's who we are."

The children looked up at her, wide-eyed around the hearth. Once the bunker had been secured, they were safe for at least a while longer. Mala took comfort in that as she fed them their soup.

"But Oma, if we all die, who will carry on the stories?" Emper's furry brows knit together in a frown as he picked at the fur on his knee. His sister put her hand over his to stop him, then looked up at Oma.

Their mother shrugged her broad shoulders. "Eventually someone will come across us, through millions of years of space travel, or through millions of years of evolution, and they'll discover our stories. It may take them generations to decipher them, but they'll learn."

Emper heaved a sigh and his sister hugged him with one arm. "It'll be okay, little brother. Death isn't scary. It's like going to sleep."

"That sounds easy," the youth said, though Eelie could tell by his downturned mouth that he was still unsure. She held onto him.

"It is easy," Oma said. "Eat your soup, Emper, and we'll share a story."

The child rallied at the promise of a story and tucked into his soup with enthusiasm. Uta, Pender, and Eelie finished theirs last.

Satisfied that the children were full from their dinners, Oma piled on more radiant stones on the hearth and let them crowd around it. With two barely out of diapers and her eldest hardly adolescent, she couldn't bear the thought of them not getting to grow up, have their own cubs, and die of old age and natural causes. No, because the Weiridians were going to ensure that they didn't, so they could spread their population at the expense of others.

As much as it put a fire in Oma's chest, she wouldn't show it. She would teach her children to fight, and she would die protecting them, but she would never let them see her weakness.

War waged overhead, and when the time came, she would kill.

"I'm going to tell you Ursala's final prophecy tonight. It was the one I told to Eelie when she came of age, but the reality is that I might die before you reach The Age, and so I'm telling you now. In case you survive."

Her four leaned in as Oma spoke.

"You know that our people will come to extinction, but we will rise again in a new form, as Ursala promised. But there will be a blood debt that the Weiridians will have to pay. For every one of us they kill, so we'll revenge upon them fifty fold. And when the Hive Mother of the Weiridians dies, so their people will die. It's in the whispers."

Oma paused when a noise scraped the bunker's roof. She poised for a fight, but then the noise stopped. When she was certain the chaos had moved on, Oma turned back to her children, who were tense with alarm, but her gentle voice lulled them back into the story.

"Ursala told us of the Distant World, Terra. On Terra, there are many climates and the planet tilts on its axis. They have warm sunshine and cold winters. Wet and dry seasons, and the people look like the snow monkeys, but without fur."

The children giggled at the bald snow monkey people and then paid attention again.

"But the one person who will exact The Vengeance for all of us is smarter than the smartest snow monkey. She is as smart as Ursala and brave as Oma, and they will call her The Judge."

Oma paused to let the cubs absorb and understand this information. "When The Judge comes, she will be broken but stubborn. She will cause a wake of chaos for herself, and she will hurt with the deepest wounds a person can ever experience. She will lose the dearest thing to her you can imagine. But she will walk. The Judge will walk into the final fight, and she will exact The Vengeance."

Overhead, shouting. The ground shook. Oma steeled herself for another bomb. It didn't come. The five were silent.

Emper warmed his hands over one of the radiant stones and sighed. "But Oma, can't The Judge come here now and kill the Hive Mother?"

Oma shook her head. "No, Emper. She lives too far away, and she might not have been born yet."

Emper's eyes welled with tears and he looked down at his feet, flat against the ground. "I don't want to die, Oma."

Their mother didn't choke up when her son began to cry—instead, she picked him up with her great strength and sat him in her lap. "I know you don't, son, and I can't think of anyone who enjoys the idea. You can't give up, Emper. You have to push forward and fight, just like your father's doing right now."

The mention of their father had an effect on all of them. Emper dried his tears in a second and the three other cubs put their arms around one another in a group hug. Eelie took the two younger ones into her lap the way that her mother did. She soothed them with nose-to-nose touches and rocked them.

"All of it will be okay, from the time we fight to the time we die. Right, Oma?"

"That's right, Eelie."

"We should go out there and fight like Daddy," Emper said, banging his fist into his other hand. "Fight alongside Daddy."

"The fight will come here, Emper, and Oma will be ready. Will you be ready?"

Emper nodded so hard his chin touched his chest. "I am ready."

Before Oma could respond, the doors crashed in and Oma turned, bellowing a roar loud enough to deafen the snake people. She knocked one down and tore into his throat with her jaws. Eelie pounced on the other, and the remaining three joined the fight.

Soon, waves of snake soldiers slithered their way in, and the bunker was overrun.

***

"That's really all I know now," Swifty said. The contents of the jar he'd sealed were almost a translucent white, with tiny hints of brown streaks running up the sides. He took the jar and gave it another shake, making some of the streaks disappear.

"The Judge—and all of this is encoded in you?" Kit shook her head and covered her eyes, resting her face against her palms.

"It's a memory. It's funny—Oma was a genius. A scientist, and that's what she chose to encode into the compound. I don't know how she did it or why she chose it, but I think her people had the gift of prophecy, too. They had the ability to perceive the future the way we perceive the past. So I think she wrote that program into the DNA so that we'd know what happened."

Kit heaved a sigh and rolled her shoulders. "I suppose, considering the fact that we've now encountered creatures from elsewhere that it's possible they could perceive the future in a way we can perceive the past. After all, *listening* isn't exactly on the radar for scientific scrutiny. I was always afraid they'd put me in the psych ward and pump me full of drugs, or worse, a lobotomy."

Swifty shook his jar again and swirled it, then let the contents settle. There were even fewer brown streaks and the bottom of the jar looked like it had a yellowing film on it. He swirled that around a couple times and set it back down once more. The yellow film turned white. "No, it's not, and I had those same fears. I just used it as best I could, whenever I could."

"Like when someone's in pain and trying to hide it," Kit said.

"That's right. That's why I became a nurse." Swifty smiled. "People said I had an instinct for it. I suppose maybe I do."

"You know I'm playing in circles, then, if you're listening."

Swifty shrugged. "You're harder to hear than the others. You put up static when I try to listen, but if you concentrate on sending your whispers, I bet it'd come in just fine."

"The Judge that Oma mentioned—it's a female, and my last name is Judge. Seems obvious, or do you think I'm being arrogant?" Kit pursed her lips to the side and sneered a bit. "I mean that question. Answer it bold."

"I don't think you're being arrogant, though that's certainly one of your flaws, especially in the past."

Kit nodded. "Agreed. I've been put in my place more times than I care to remember."

"You suffered the loss of your son for it, and that's what humbled you." Swifty looked into her eyes.

"Yes. It humbled me, but it didn't make me timid."

"And that's what we need right now, Doc. We need you bold." Swifty waved his hand to the back of the wagon. "Back there in Platt's Gulch, they're waiting for you to destroy the Hive Mother. They're in hiding."

"You know this from the whispers?" Kit started to stand up, then forced herself back down.

"That and while you were recovering in the wagon at night, I sneaked back to the town to try to help. People are waiting for you. The people you cured are preparing for the fight of their lives. Most are just trying to go about their business under the snake people's rule."

"So this Hive Mother—she's still alive?"

Swifty took a stick from his back pocket, and a knife, and began to whittle off a sharp point. "Yep. Bet you can guess who it is, too."

Kit scowled and her eyes narrowed. "Yina."

"Yina. Disguised as the Deputy."

"A shapeshifter, then, like Deringer." Kit shook her head. "Incredible."

"She must've killed the real Yina and then took her form, and no one ever noticed. Yina was a woman who kept to herself for the most part, and people didn't know what to look for to tell that she'd changed." Swifty kept whittling while he spoke. "Yina went from a cool, distant woman to a cool, distant woman who took occasional interest in others."

"So everyone just thought she was trying to warm up, then." The doctor put a hand to her lips and traced the dry outline, feeling bumps and cracks in the midst of their healing.

"You got it," Swifty put the sharpened stick down by the jar and folded up his knife. "No one ever knew the difference."

"That means—but I shot her in the eye, didn't I?" Kit sat forward and slapped her fist against her knee. "That's what kills them, doesn't it?"

Swifty held up his hands. "Yes, Doc, that's what kills them, but you have to shoot out both eyes or they can heal. They regenerate."

Kit smacked her forehead. "Of course they do. Of-fucking-course they do. They must have some reptilian features, so regeneration is one of them." She gave an exasperated moan. "If only I'd not let that other one stop me."

"They're drones. They protect the Hive Mother."

Kit nodded. "Funny how insectile that is for a reptilian race."

"It's odd to me, too, but considering we have virus and fish ancestry, I can't say it's a surprise." Swifty pulled two cigarettes from his pouch and offered Kit one. She waved her hand in a 'no thanks' gesture and he put one away, lighting his own. A cloud of gray ballooned, pushing itself out flat into the wagon. "But let me ask you something, Doc."

Kit looked up from examining the contents of Swifty's jar. The brown streaks were entirely gone now and the mixture was white, like milk. "What's your question?"

"When you try to *listen* to the snake people, what do you hear?"

"Static. Like on the wireless in the middle of the night. Sometimes I think I hear a voice, but I can't get it to tune."

"Same here. With humans, I can get the reception. With the snake things, I get static."

Kit shook her head. "I get that with humans, too, sometimes. Have all my life."

"You sure they're human?"

The breath rushed from Kit as if she'd been hit in the stomach. *You sure they're human?*

A sea of faces from her journey from Charles Town crowded into her mind's eye. It seemed that so many of them gave off static. "No, Slater. Now I'm not so sure. But that means—that means they're everywhere."

Swifty nodded. "I got thinking about that last night. How many of them are here, on Terra, waiting to wipe us out?"

"I can't begin to count," Kit said, then growled under her breath. "An entire population that probably rivals our armed forces, not to mention their technology."

"They're hiding, waiting for their signal, whatever it is."

"From Yina. Platt's Gulch is a testing facility." Kit licked her lips and Swifty reached into his pouch, handing her a salve. She took it and applied it.

"It's most likely."

"We have to stop Yina from doing this, then. If we kill her, then we'll eliminate them all, according to what Oma said about Ursala's prophecy."

"That's what she said. Judge."

Kit ran her hand through her hair. "Easy, simple, no pressure at all."

"You have a gift for sarcasm."

"It's the best feature I have." Kit shook her head. "I wish they'd killed her in the first place." She thought about it for a moment, wondering how Yina managed to avoid it during the war on their own planet.

Swifty sighed. "Well, it's up to you. You're the one who has to kill her—so how do you plan to go about it?"

"Whatever I plan, it won't go well, I'm sure." Kit shrugged. "That's how it always happens, right?"

"Seems that way sometimes," he said. "Most of the time." He laughed at Kit's raised eyebrow. "Okay, all of the time pretty much."

Kit laughed in spite of herself. "My plans are to go into town and attempt to hide out on the roof at Polly's, and when Yina comes to the Sheriff's Office and does her usual looking up at the clock tower, I'll be there to make sure she gets an eyeful."

Swifty thought about this, then put up his hands and spread his fingers. "You know what? That'll work, but we've got to think about things that could go wrong. Like getting you back into town undetected."

"Do they think I'm dead?"

Swifty nodded. “They think you’re dead. They know I’m alive, and I’ve got a bounty on my head.”

“You’ve got a bounty and you keep going back?” Kit raised her eyebrows at him. “Come on, Slater, that’s not bright.”

“I know it’s not, but to save your life, it was worth the risk to go back. You have to fulfill the prophecy. I thought you would that day when you were set to hang, but the prophecy didn’t mention The Judge would get shot.”

“Inconvenient, these prophecies. But a shame we don’t have them here. I’d like to see if I actually succeed in this task.”

“That, Doc, is the only thing I can foresee—if I help.”

They were quite for awhile, just swimming in their oceans of thoughts. Kit began to wander into the sea of what ifs, making tiny adjustments to her plans. What if they were detected? She’d have to improvise.

She could do that.

“I’m tired, Slater. I don’t think I’m fully healed yet. Tomorrow I’ll be better.”

“Yes you will. I have a fresh batch of mozhuatil that says so. But you need to rest. You can sleep here in the wagon. A short siesta followed by some dinner will help you get right again."

Kit hunkered down and unfurled her bedroll, then stretched out on it.

"A short siesta, that sounds good," she said, then turned over on her side. "When I get up, I'll hunt for dinner, how about that?"

Swifty smiled. "Sounds fair, Doc. I'll build the fire."

She closed her eyes and drifted into a world of endless consequences.

***

Waking to the sounds of Swifty clattering about in the wagon, Kit looked at her pocket watch. She'd only slept for an hour, but the feeling of cleansing and renewal took over her body. Swifty handed her a bowl of the mozhuatil and she drank it. "This batch tastes sweeter."

"That's because your body is getting less dependent on it to heal you, now," Swifty said. "Once you drink that, I don't think you'll need anymore. But if you get a feeling like you do, tell me, and you can have more."

"It's not addictive, is it?" Kit stopped drinking and looked up at the nurse, brows raised with concern.

"Not at all, although the sedative side effect is nice, that goes away after a couple weeks. You'll be just fine."

Accepting this, Kit drank the rest of the bowl and set it aside, then checked her pistol. "I'll go get us something. Seen anything good?"

"Couple quail and some jackrabbits. Big hares, couple of roadrunners. Not bad for a warm day."

Kit nodded and made her way out of the wagon, hopping down onto the sandy ground. She took a look around, not only for animals, but for others—for snake people and perhaps human allies or slaves, if any.

Once she was sure it was secure, Kit headed for the brush to flush out quail, or even jackrabbits.

Even when she was young, she'd always enjoyed shooting. Her father and mother often shot for sport, with clay pigeons and occasionally one of them would go on a game hunt. They rarely failed to have Kathryn with them, learning about the hunt and not just shooting animals for sport. They taught her respect for her prey, and that sometimes, the prey became the predator. A large buck could gore a person with ease, and it was always wise to keep her eyes focused on her surroundings.

She did the same here, and every sense came to life. She could smell the desert flowers open and blossoming as if she had her nose stuck in them. The sounds of animals—every tick, scrape, and patter of tiny feet in the brush was a symphony in her ears. The sun, darkening in its fall to the horizon, gave the scrub a gray-blue tinge, and Kit felt as though she could see every blade, every leaf, every inch of bramble.

The doctor picked up a stone and rolled it into the brush with one hand, revolver at the ready in the other. A pair of quail and three jackrabbits came scurrying out, and Kit took her best shots.

One, two, three—two quail fell and one jackrabbit followed suit. She hurried over to them to make sure they didn't suffer to become dinner, and when she was certain they were dead, she collected them in her rucksack.

Doctor Judge did not smile at her success. Instead, she carried on back to the campground, rucksack bulging with her game. There was little point in looking to her past, so with each step, she made plans for her future. What she would do to fight Yina, how she would improvise should she be caught. Her draw was quick—she practiced plenty for these days though she never realized it—but Yina may be quicker the next time around, and she may have more drones to guard her.

She wasn't about to let her guard down, and she doubted Yina would, too. Even if Yina thought Kathryn was dead, it didn't mean that she should be careless. There were others that could kill her—such as Slater.

It would have to be by her hand. *Their prophecy said as much.*

"Bah, prophecies," Kit said in the wind as she saw Swifty ahead, making a big fire for the evening. He looked up as if he heard her, and waved, smiling. She waved back and kept walking.

As she reached the circle of stones, the doctor set down her rucksack and pulled out the rabbit and quail. "I'm pretty hungry, having not eaten since this morning," she said, patting her stomach. "I don't store it—I burn it."

Swifty chuckled. "I'm the same way. Mama always used to tell me I'd waste away if I skipped a meal."

"And was she right?" Kit grinned as she started to take the feathers off one of the quail. Swifty got to work on skinning the rabbit.

"A little bit. I mean, it's impossible to skip a meal, so they say."

Kit nodded. "True, but if you didn't compensate by eating more, later, did you lose weight?"

"Like a shot."

"Keep eating, then. A whole bird for each of us, and we can split the jackrabbit."

They cleaned the animals in silence.

After dinner, the two shared smokes, and Swifty made coffee.

"I find it's easier to wake up in the morning if I drink it right before bed," he said. "You, Doc?"

Kit nodded. "About the same." She rolled her cigarette between her fingers and produced a match from her pocket so fast that it looked like she'd summoned fire out of the air. Swifty gave an appreciative whistle.

"I gotta ask, Doc. Where'd you learn all that sleight-of-hand? You're a quick shot and you managed to escape those knots. Polly was impressed with your tricks when you first met, too." Swifty grinned. "Would you show me one?"

The doctor reached forward and Swifty leaned into her, and she pulled a book of matches from behind his ear. "Is that enough of one?"

Swifty laughed and took the proffered matchbook, lighting his own cigarette. "I'll admit it, Doc—it's not enough. Back in the hospital, when the kids were sick, sometimes you'd show them a special magic trick or with cards and such, and I loved it. Like the puzzle book in little Willie's ear. Made me feel like a little boy all over again."

"I think that's how magic tricks make us all feel. We're skeptics. We know what we see is a trick, but that doesn't seem to make the delight of a well-played one fade. At least not to me." Kit dragged from her cigarette and blew a smoke ring, put her finger in it, and made a pull-down motion. In her hand, a small gold nugget appeared. She handed that to Swifty.

He took it with another grin. "I know that they're tricks, of course, but I never knew how they work. Where'd you learn them?"

Kit stretched her legs out in front of her and angled them away from the fire. "My father and mother. Father was the one who taught me coin and card tricks, and

Mother taught me escape artistry. She actually learned from her parents, and had to use it a few times in her life."

"Really?" Swifty's eyes went wide. "I didn't think the East was so untamed."

The doctor laughed. "Well, she was from a prominent Albion family and was held for ransom on a few occasions in her life. Since her parents refused to negotiate and taught her skills she needed, she got herself out of the mess each time."

"Seems like you come from a long line of fighters, Doc." Swifty took a drag from his cigarette and examined the small gold nugget. He tried to hand it back to Kit, but the doctor held up her hand.

"I do. You keep it, Slater. Payment for your life-saving services, though I owe you much more than that."

Swifty gave her a bashful grin and put the money in his pocket. "You know, Doc, I had a thought."

"Oh?"

"You had to use your magic to get out of the hangman's noose—so I guess you and your mother have that in common."

Kit smiled gently. "I suppose we do, Slater. I suppose we do."

They smoked as a lull came over them, bellies digesting their large dinners. Kit noted the soreness in her midsection vanished. The concoction that Slater had put together seemed to do more to the cells. It was something worth studying, but now was not the time.

When her cigarette wore down to a nub, the doctor pitched it into the fire and inhaled the sweet smell of the tobacco as it burned. Shortly after, Swifty did the same with his leftover cigarette. Kit looked up at the stars, finding the constellations and remembering their stories. Felis Catus, sitting in front of a pond where Pisces leapt from the water. The night cooled enough so that the doctor could see her breath. She pulled her duster around herself, enjoying the nip in the air.

"At first, I had a kind of crush on you, Doc."

Kit looked over at Swifty and gave a light shrug. "It happens."

"But now, I see you more like—a mama."

The doctor smiled. "That's a nice thing to say, Slater. But why are you telling me this?"

Swifty bit his lower lip, and for a moment, it looked like he regretted saying anything. The young man took a deep breath and seemed to muster up some courage. "Well, Doc. I mean, if one of us dies—or we both do—I wanted you to know that and that I think highly of you."

The doctor put her hand on Swifty's ankle and gave it a squeeze. "Thanks, Slater. You're not such a bad guy, yourself."

"Gee, that's right kind of you to say, Doc."

They chuckled and Kit stood up. "Time for bed, Slate."

"Yes, ma'am."

She unrolled her bed and climbed inside, pulling the blanket over her shoulder and setting her hat down harder on her head, over her eyes. In the blackness, sleep came fast.

***

Before dawn revealed pink and gold hues on the horizon, Kit sat up and looked around, feeling a weight on her foot, over her boots. She plucked the blanket away, expecting to see a snake or two coiled around her feet, but sighed with relief when she saw it was just Swifty's arms, still attached to the stretched-out Swifty.

"Wake up, princess," Kit said, nudging his arms with gentle taps. "We've got to get into town today, and quick, before sun-up."

Swifty stirred and looked up at the doctor. "Princess? Really?"

"Really. Come on, let's go." Kit stood up and headed for the brush. "I'll be back in a moment. Get some of the food set up for breakfast and then we'll sneak into Platt's Gulch."

After breakfast, Swifty set about making their camp safe from outsiders by boobytrapping the wagon. They took their belongings and set out on foot towards the Twist River.

"The best way to get into town is through the tunnel—back before they made cannabis legal again, there was a whole underground network to run the green from East to West. Thing is, Yina doesn't seem to know about it, so she doesn't have any guards down there."

Kit gave him a funny look. "No one ever mentioned that before."

"Towns have secrets. All of them," Swifty shrugged. "Wasn't important until today, anyway."

The doctor nodded. “I suppose that’s true.” She gave him a measured look. “This self-assured Slater is different, but I like him.”

Swifty gave her an ‘aw, shucks’ grin, and Kit chuckled at the circles of color flooding into his cheeks.

They walked together along the edge of the Twist river until they crossed a narrow footbridge. Across from the bridge, a set of brambles and brush greeted them. The thicket looked natural enough, and Kit tried to figure out how to get across it.

That’s when she spied something shining. Glinting by the light of Swifty’s lamp. He reached down and lifted it. A handle.

“I’ve got to do a better job of hiding this entrance next time,” Swifty said. “Luckily you can only see it from this close and not from inside the town.” Once it was open, he stood back. “Hop in, Doc. It’s a short drop and there’s a ladder, too.”

Kit wasted no time getting into the square hole in the ground and climbing the ladder down until it ended. Swifty was right: it was a short drop. She extended her arms and made a soft landing, looking around in the semi-darkness and making room for Swifty to join her.

The rush of the river overhead, and occasional liquid drops into small pools greeted her. A smell of chalk and salt filled her nose.

"Doesn't look like there's anything but one route to follow," the doctor reached into her rucksack and took out her own lamp. "This will lead to Polly's?"

"Polly's, the hospital, and Overton's Feed & Farm Supply," Swifty said, voice low.

"All the places you could trade cannabis—of course," Kit said with a nod. "Lead the way, Slater."

They followed the narrow path straight for a short period, then stopped at the fork that branched into three directions. Swifty pointed at the fork on the left.

"That's the route to Polly's. Straight and bending to the right is the hospital, and the one all the way on the right is Overton's." Swifty wiped sweat from his forehead. Though the morning was cool, underground in the close quarters, it was just the opposite. The moisture made it almost like a sauna.

Kit put her hand on her revolver and tipped her hat back. "Let's go, then."

Following the route to Polly's, they came upon a step down into a basement area that seemed to be a dead end. Barrels of old whiskey and boxes that used to contain goods for the saloon lined the walls. Just three walls and the path leading back out into the tunnels.

"It's a good illusion," the doctor spoke in a hoarse whisper. "The wall here, I mean." She ran her hand along the stone's surface. It was drier than it looked. In the corner, she felt some bumps and cracks. Swifty nodded at her.

"Yeah, you got it, Doc. Just push on those three bumps and it'll give."

She did, and it did. The wall moved just an inch, and then slid to the side in a rush that made a whisper in the darkness.

The opening was straight into Polly's storeroom, with fresher crates and barrels lining the walls, and the smell of sawdust and oak wafting from the floor. Kit repressed a sneeze and put her sleeve to her nose. Swifty closed the door behind them by pulling on a chain on the inside of the room. It made a light click, then all was quiet.

Swifty and the doctor stood there, listening for any sounds around them that might signify trouble, but all they could hear was the scrape and bang of pots and pans, light footsteps in the galley, and Polly humming now and then. The corners of Kit's mouth upturned slightly.

After a few minutes of listening to the noises around them, Swifty went up to the door and did a series of knocks. Rap, rap, rap—rap rap—rap, rap, rap—then stood back and waited.

A single set of footsteps clattered down a flight of stairs, closer and closer. Then nothing.

Rap, rap.

Swifty nodded and gave Kit the thumb's up, then knocked three times back.

The door opened and Polly gasped at the sight of the doctor. She repressed a squeal which made it sound more like a leaky faucet. The woman wrapped her arms around Kit and stood on tiptoe to plant a kiss on her lips.

Kit didn't stiffen to the touch, but returned the embrace. She let Polly kiss her, too stunned to return that.

"Ooh I'm just so glad you're alive, Doc," Polly said when she let go. "Swifty said you were but for awhile I didn't believe him."

"Believe it," Kit said, looking down at Polly with a grin. Swifty gave her a knowing look and she shook her head at him, then turned back to the woman. "I bet that breakfast is good. I can smell the bacon all the way down here."

Polly laughed. "I'll fix you a plate, Doc."

"You'll have to fix it for me later," Kit said. "I need to get up on your rooftop and do a little hunting."

The three went inside and Kit made her way upstairs. Swifty stayed with Polly in the kitchen, and the doctor took the back stairs up to the rooftop.

Once there, she set up an area that had a structural blind, but one that only blocked the view inside. From Kit's vantage point, she could see the Sheriff's Office in the gold and orange tones of the dawn.

Kit would be patient. All there was to do now was wait for Yina to stroll up Main Street and head into the office—however long that took. There, Kit would take her shots for the eyes.

While the morning felt cool in comparison to the heat of the underground passages, it was warming with each tick of the doctor's pocket watch. Yina was bound to make her approach soon, and Kit was ready for her.

Hours passed and the sun climbed high, making the day's heat strong, but Kit could bear it. It was dry enough. She wanted water, but didn't dare take her eyes off the Sheriff's office as she searched for Yina.

The town was devoid of townsfolk—streets quiet, no business taking place, and it made Judge snarl with contempt over what these visitors were turning the town into. Their conquistador ways were hopelessly outdated, and they deserved nothing but her contempt.

A cloud of dust caught the doctor's attention and she turned her sharp blue eyes to the horizon. Yina rode her horse into town, down Main Street at a breaking gallop. She had a rifle strapped to her back and was leaning down on the horse, as if she could meld into it.

That's when Kit saw the other two approaching behind her, though their horses weren't as breakneck as Yina's. She brought her horse to a skidding stop and whistled.

The static that filled Kit's head was so strong her vision doubled and began to bounce as though she were riding a horse, herself. A wave of nausea overcame her and she doubled over, mentally putting up a wall around her mind. Envisioning a fortress of protection. The sound stopped, and Kit felt the familiar burn and trickle in her nostrils. She pinched them closed and leaned forward.

Still clutching her gun, the doctor peered over her blind at the sight below. Yina was standing in front of the Sheriff's office with her back to Kit, tending the three horses and tying them to their posts. The two drones, however, were missing.

It didn't take long for Kit to figure out they were inside Polly's, because the doors to the saloon banged open, and Polly and Swifty came out, dragged by the drones. Both were shouting and hollering, and Polly was trying to swing and kick at them. But the drones were too strong for that, and managed to hold her.

"Kathryn Judge," Yina called out to the empty street, "unless you want your beloved ones to die, you'd better show yourself and surrender."

At that, Kit stood up. "I'll show myself, Yina, but I won't surrender."

"Then your friends will die," Yina said, waving her hands at the two allies below.

The doctor holstered her weapon, hopped down onto the eaves, then slid down one of the posterns, landing just in front of the horse trough. She needed a distraction.

That distraction was provided by a loud hum. Not just a hum that filled the air with sound, but a deep, low rumbling hum that made all their chests vibrate and penetrated their minds. Kit could hear the hum not just from the outside, but from inside.

There, at high noon, a hum so loud it seemed to make the breeze pick up. The horses nickered nervous concerns to each other. The drones looked around to pinpoint the source.

But there was no source. It was coming from every direction.

The focal point was the doctor. (The Judge.)

"That's her—that's the one," Yina said to her drones. "Kill her."

The drones pushed Swifty and Polly to the side. The humming intensified. Polly and Swifty clutched one another and ducked behind a rain barrel. They were covering their ears.

"You know I'm The Judge," Kit said. "You know that can't happen."

"The prophecy is a lie made up to tell babies who knew they were on their way to extinction. You'll do the same, *Judge*." Yina laughed. "You're outnumbered, outgunned. Once I kill you and feast on your heart, Kathryn, I'll make Swifty my slave and Polly will hang."

Kit gave her a smile that was almost a sneer. "Doesn't do to tell your enemy your plans, Yina. Where do you suppose that humming is coming from? That a coincidence? That something you made happen?"

Six shots, six eyes.

I am The Judge.

They drew their side arms and Yina made a grab for her rifle. Kit felt that hum wash over her into a moment where time seemed to slow to a sloth's pace.

Six shots, six eyes.

Her hand went to her weapon and she drew, as if her hand knew exactly how to move to take aim. She had no gun. Her hand was the gun—her fingers were the trigger, her thumb, the hammer.

In a fluid movement, she shelled out six shots, and her aim was sure.

Six shots, no eyes—not anymore.

The eyes popped and bloodied with each report, crimson oil weeping in fountains as the two drones took their measure first, falling to the ground in twitching spasms. Yina aimed her rifle, but couldn't fire fast enough.

One eye out, two eyes out, and the humming grew. The ground shook.

From the foothills, echoes of screams both audible and telepathic filled the town as the hum grew to a feverish chant.

"What we've become, so have you—what we've become, so have you—"

As Yina twitched and rolled about on the ground in pools of her own blood, spasms growing more and more faint, along with the screams. When the Hive Mother stopped moving, the screams went out altogether.

When the screaming died, the humming lowered, then ceased.

The Judge walked over to the body and tapped it with her boot. Yina's corpse rolled, and mutated into her true form—another snake-like creature, but with a reptile crown on top of her head, a red-orange crest with spikes on the end.

"Sure as Perdition, I was right this time," she looked up and around. "But I wasn't alone—you're all listeners, aren't you?"

Faces started peeking out of windows, and people—Kit's former patients—came out in little groups. Some held hands. Some held each other. Swifty joined them.

"Well, you killed them alone—we just made it stick," Swifty said.

"I'm glad for it—and humbled by it." Kit reached out to Swifty and put her hand on his shoulder. "I couldn't have done it by myself."

Swifty clutched Kit's hand and took it in both of his. "You didn't, it's true, but when you have allies, you don't need to do everything on your own."

Kit nodded. "So I've learned."

THE JUDGE'S LAST

A sea of barbecue and picnic foods crowded the tables laid out on Main Street under tents to keep the food in the shade. Light breezes carried the chatter of excited townsfolk through to the band playing lively jazz tunes. There were men in red and white striped suitcoats and white linen pants serving up corn on the cob and plates of ribs to the attendees. Children ran around and chased each other, giggling as they went.

Kit took a look around at the townspeople, alone in her corner with a plate of rib bones and cobs left behind. She watched the children play and the people socialize in a much-needed celebration. They had survived. They buried their dead. Now, they were ready to move forward and make peace.

Rice was gone, along with his penitents. When the Hive Mother died, so did Rice, and his followers, unsure of what to do, left town to find another mad hatter to guide them down their distorted paths. Some came to the hospital, looking for answers, looking for forgiveness.

"We feel like we were under a spell," Elias Crane, a bespectacled small man said. His wife, Joanna, nodded with enthusiasm.

"Could you ever forgive us our transgressions?"

"I can't provide you with forgiveness. But your remorse is an opportunity." She reached into the desk drawer and pulled out pamphlets and a book. "This here is a primer on scientific method, and the pamphlets are about varieties of illness and how they form."

She pushed the literature into their hands. "Read. Learn. Redeem yourselves through education rather than speculation. When you don't understand something, perhaps learn about it rather than fear it so much you give up your good senses."

Kit sent them on their way. *You have to work forgiveness out for yourselves,* she thought.

The doctor rolled a cigarette between her thumb and forefinger, tightening its seal. She put it between her lips and lit it with a match.

Tap.

Kit turned to see a child with wide brown eyes and a shock of black hair staring up at her. In tiny, fat hands, a deck of cards. He handed them to her as several other children gathered around to see what was happening.

"What's this about?" The doctor asked, blowing her smoke upward, away from the children's faces.

"Nurse Slater says you do magic with cards," the boy said, holding the cards up to her face as best he could. "Dale Spivey said so, too."

Kit chuckled. "Did they, now?" She puffed on her cigarette and took the pack out of the boy's hand. "Okay, Fabiano. Let's see if I can make *you* do magic, instead."

The young boy looked skeptical, but interested. Kit fanned out the deck with one hand and took her cigarette from her mouth with the other. "Pick a card and show it to your friends, but don't show me, okay? And don't say what it is out loud."

Fabiano picked a card and did as she told him.

"Good. Now hand it to me, face down." She put the cigarette back in her mouth and let the boy put the card back. She shuffled the deck, keeping her eye on the right card.

"Okay, cut the deck."

Some adults came to look in on the spectacle as excited and wide-eyed as the children were. Kit kept watching the deck. “Take the half on your left.”

Fabiano had to think about it for a moment, but chose the one Kit pointed out. She shuffled the cards and cut them with one hand, then offered them to Fabiano. “Pick any ten cards from that deck.”

He picked his ten.

“Now pick five.”

He picked five.

“Throw those five away, and put your hand on one of these five left.” Kit took a drag from her cigarette while he did this, feigning that she wasn’t really looking at the marked card.

Fabiano looked up at her, and she nodded. “That’s your card, isn’t it?”

He picked it up and showed it to the crowd, a look of delight crossing his round features. Excited and forgetful, he threw his arms around Kit and hugged her hard. The doctor gasped and picked him up off the ground, hugging him back with almost as much force.

"You really are magic," the boy said, nearly breathless. Kit laughed.

"Someday you'll learn the tricks. But not with that thing in your ear." She pulled a coin from his ear and handed it to him. "Here. Go to Appleton's and ask Mister Braxbury for a sarsaparilla and a book called *One Thousand Magic Tricks*. That'll get you started."

Fabiano gasped, then ran off with his friends chasing him towards Appleton's Pharmacy and Chemist. Some of the adults clapped, and Kit waved them off with a shake of her head and a laugh.

"Thank your genetics for those quick hands," Swifty said from behind her. Kit twisted to look up at him and he came into view, sitting down in the corner with her. She gave him a measured look.

"I'd say fastest hands in the West, but I've heard about Polly's tricks," she said. Swifty laughed and the doctor chuckled over seeing another faint blush rise to his face.

"What are you doing over here, all alone?" Swifty asked. He motioned for one of Polly's boys to come over with a tray of desserts and took two slices of huckleberry pie, handing one of the plates to Kit.

The server dished out two forks and excused himself. Kit stamped out her cigarette in her rib plate.

"There's a banquet in your honor, Judge, and here you are, set down in the corner at the edge of the tent by your lonesome." Swifty took a bite of pie and gave a nod of approval. "What's that all about?"

Kit shrugged. "This isn't for me, Slater. It's for all of us—for everything the town went through together. I can't take all the credit for saving the town. It was everyone. Those who stayed to fight. Those who died in the process. You and the lives we saved together. The people who became listeners, even if it was temporary. It's not about me. It's about Platt's Gulch."

She stuck her fork in the slice of pie and examined the contents, then took a hesitant bite. The taste, similar to blueberry, burst on her tongue. Experimental taste a success, she took another bite.

"It is about all of us, Doc, but like it or not, you're a part of us now, and we're gonna celebrate every minute we have you here. There are five doctors coming from the East to help staff the hospital, and soon, this'll be a place where you can settle down. Make a life for yourself." Swifty took another bite of pie.

"I can't, Slater. Not yet. I made a promise to someone, and I intend to keep it. I already told Polly. She was sore at me for leaving till I explained why. I hope you won't be too upset with me, either." Kit pulled a map out of her duster pocket, and a small, black velvet cloth came out with it. She set the map on the table and moved her half-eaten pie to the side. "Hope Falls. I promised Gemini I'd go there for her, and I intend to keep my promise."

Swifty nodded. "I understand, Doc. I figured you weren't going to stay much longer. That's why we rushed to put something together for you—for when you're ready to leave."

"I'm leaving by sunset, Slater. I might be back someday, but I'll have to go where I'm needed. Where I'm called. Not by some supernatural force, but by the whispers. And the whispers are saying I need to go to Hope Falls." Kit folded up her map and put the velvet-encased stone in her pocket.

"Someday, huh? Might never see you again." Swifty frowned, and Kit thought she saw his eyes shine.

"Maybe not, but I'll come back if you need me. The whispers will guide me back."

"They always guide us," Carmen's voice came from behind them. "They guided me here, now."

Kit turned to see the woman, still looking frail but recovered, and motioned her over. Carmen sat down with her own plate full of pie.

"I knew you could do it. The whispers knew, too."

The doctor gave Carmen a curious look. "How did the whispers know? They predict the future?"

Carmen shook her head. "The M'aqual don't believe that time is a straight line. It allows us to listen to whispers from all directions."

"I'd have nosebleeds for decades," Kit said.

"No you wouldn't. And maybe someday you won't have that problem," Carmen shrugged. "Someday you won't resist the whispers so hard, and you'll understand what I mean."

They were silent as they finished their slices of pie together, then Swifty stood and patted her arm. She let him.

But he didn't leave. Instead, he tapped a water glass and stood on his chair and Kit looked up at him, mouth open to protest, then closed again as she could see he wasn't about to listen to her.

"Friends, fellow Gulchers, may I please have your attention?" Swifty gathered a little crowd of people and Kit sat in stunned silence, composing herself as well as she could. Once satisfied that people were paying the doctor and him rapt attention, he continued.

"Today marks a sad but joyous occasion—where we recognize The Judge—Doctor Kathryn Judge, as the one who came into Platt's Gulch expecting nothing, but giving everything to help save our town. We mourn the dead, celebrate the living, and say goodbye to our Walking Doctor. May she keep walking to where she's needed."

The crowd echoed a 'hear, hear' and praise for the doctor as they toasted her with glasses of wine, whiskey, and water.

Kit bit her lower lip as someone began a chant: "Speech! Speech!"

She stood and raised her glass to the crowd. "I'm not good at speeches so I'll keep this brief: take care of each other, and of yourselves. Remember that you are the ones who pulled together in a time of crisis, and you are the backbone of this town."

"Hear, hear!" the crowd responded and some applauded. Others clinked their glasses. Kathryn set down her glass and put one hand to her heart as she faced Swifty. "I'll be on my way."

Gathering her rucksack and making sure she had everything on her, she left the tent and started up Main Street, heading towards the Western Foothills. The Charlie River would lead her to the best path for Hope Falls.

"Doc, wait a minute—we have something for you," Polly's voice caught Kit's attention and she turned to look at the woman, who was walking along side Yaja. The older woman guided a flawless black mare to her.

"This is Tilly, Doc," Yaja introduced the horse. "She lost her foal to a pack of feral dogs last year, and since then she's been wandering. No one's been able to catch her."

"Not till you came into town," Polly said. "Overton told us she's been docile ever since, and her owners are long gone from the illness, before you even came here. So we decided she'd make a nice gift for you. It's as if she'd been waiting for you."

Yaja offered Kit the reins, and for a moment, the doctor stood, stunned at the magnificent beast they'd offered her as a gift.

"She comes with thirty acres if you want it," Swifty said. A small crowd gathered around as he spoke, watching the doctor and Tilly with bright interest.

Kit smiled and put her hand over her chest. "Give the land to anyone who needs it. Tilly and I have something in common. Perhaps she knows that."

The horse took a step forward and Kit put her hand on the young mare's muzzle. Tilly nudged, and put her head down to Kit's, touching foreheads.

I remember you, sweet girl.

"She's saddled and ready for you. Got bags of feed on her if there's nowhere to graze, but if you're headed to Hope Falls, there'll be plenty along the way." Polly's eyes shined as she spoke and her smile seemed a little forced, but her whispers were genuine.

I'm going to miss what could've been, Doc.

Kit put her arms around Polly and pressed her lips to the other woman's. The crowd made oohing noises and a few applauded. When they parted, the doctor "It'll be fine,

Polly, don't dwell on me for a minute." She turned to the crowd once more. "Remember the dead. Fight for the living."

Breaking the embrace, the doctor—The Judge—turned to Swifty and hugged him goodbye, then mounted the mare, who accepted her rider without so much as a nicker.

And as the sun made its journey down below the horizon, The Walking Doctor rode off for her fortunes in Hope Falls.

EPILOGUE

With one hand, Kathryn pressed the smooth river stone into the bed among rocks that had similar shape and appearance. "There, Gemini. I did as you promised. I'm sorry I failed you once, but glad I didn't fail you twice."

Tilly, who was drinking from the gin clear river, stuck her head up and looked at the doctor for a moment, then went back to drinking. Kit stood up straight and put her hands on her hips, looking around at the chalk falls. The place was a verdant paradise with its lush plant life and edible flora.

The doctor came up alongside the horse. "I'm upriver from you, so I'll have a drink. But don't you dare void in the water, Tilly, or I'll send you back to Platt's Gulch."

Tilly gave her a sidelong glance and stopped drinking, then marched off to munch on some Esther grass. Kit chuckled and bent down again, washing her face in the cold water and drinking handfuls. It was clean, filtered by the chalk, and at the head of the spring, there was nothing to pollute it.

So she drank, filled her canteens, then bathed.

The cool river washed her off and she swam to the sunnier parts of the water, enjoying the warmth the sunshine provided. With the past city cleaned from her body, she splashed and played with the water, letting it soothe her.

Her heart ached for her son to be there with her, and it always would, but today, she was accepting of it. This would be as close to peace as the doctor could find. "And that's enough," she said to the rocks jutting out of the water.

Some of the stones were flat-topped and looked like a good place for sitting. As Kit looked around and watched Tilly run around without her saddle, she swam over to the area and examined them. On a whim, she placed her hand against the one that looked like a chair, and stretched her mind into the past. What her parents thought was a vivid imagination, Kit understood to be a gift. Thanks to Carmen, she knew.

The whispers were quiet, but she heard one familiar voice underneath all the others who sat here before.

I'll be back someday, the whisper said.

A single drop of blood ran out of Kit's nose and she sniffed it up and away. Ever since Swifty gave her that restorative concoction, the nosebleeds had faded to just a drop or two. Another thing Carmen had been right about. It would take work and time, but perhaps she could get them to stop entirely.

She really had to stretch her mind far to get them started—like looking into past whispers. Past memories that the rocks seemed to absorb. She didn't dare stretch to the future. Not yet, but she wondered what the stones could tell her, just the same.

"That's an unscientific thought," Kit said, then laughed. Tilly looked over at her and whinnied, then came back to the river for another drink.

The doctor swam to meet her and walked out of the water. It was a soothing place, though perhaps not as much as the beaches had once been, but it was enough.

While she was dressing once more and drying off, she sat back on a rock formation, wondering and imagining that Gemini once did this same thing here, but didn't reach out for any whispers this time. She didn't want to push it. She imagined they were bound by the spring. The water connected them in life and death.

Kit pulled her locket out of her duster's inner pocket and opened it, gazing at the picture of her boy. She closed it and clutched it to her chest, then put the chain around her neck, clasping it in the back. It was lighter without the vial, but it stuck to her chest, above her heart. She put on her shirt and ran a comb through her hair, then settled back on the smooth rock formation. After she was finished dressing, the doctor looked up at the bright blue sky and gazed at the clouds. Some were high up and hazy, and the sky poked right through them. Some were fat and fluffy, and Kit let her mind wander, making the shapes into recognizable objects. A jackrabbit. A galloping horse. The sea anemones that Thomas used to pick up and hug before setting them back in the water. Kit laughed at the memory from when he was small. Though there were times it stung too hard to even think about him, today wasn't that day. Instead, she remembered him for him, and not for the absence of him.

The sting was not so acute, and she pulled the memories around her like a comforting blanket, and let herself remember her son.

Those memories turned to other thoughts and daydreams as the doctor cloud gazed, and she closed her eyes, resting the back of her head on a smooth dip in the stone. The sun warmed her dark hair and helped it dry. Tilly nickered, but sounded more and more distant. Kit sighed and soaked in the solitude.

Please, Mister, don't hurt me. Oh I hope he won't hurt me again—

He's gonna leave us to die here, I just know it—

I'm praying to you, Alastor. Please. If you really exist, save me from the monster, please, please, please—

Where is my son? Where are the children?

I can't find them, they're going to hang me if I can't find them.

Kit finished getting dressed and heaved a long sigh. "Well, Tilly—break's over. Hope Falls is in need of a doctor—or a judge."

The horse, upon hearing her name, meandered over to Kit and let the doctor affix her saddle, bridle and bit, then allowed Kit to mount her again. They rode off in the direction of the town, heeding the call of the helpless, the vulnerable.

End

www.ingramcontent.com/pod-product-compliance
Lightning Source LLC
Chambersburg PA
CBHW030538310726
48979CB00010B/1958/J

* 9 7 8 1 9 6 3 9 7 0 0 9 8 *